STRONG at the BROKEN PLACES

David Doucette

NIMBUS
PUBLISHING

Nimbus Publishing Limited
PO Box 9166
Halifax, NS   B3K 5M8
(902) 455-4286

Cover photo: Mark Simkins Photography
Interior design: Margaret Issenman, MGDC

Printed and bound in Canada

Canadian Cataloguing in Publication Data

     Doucette, David
     Strong at the broken places: a novel

     ISBN 1-55109-361-8

I. Title.

PS 8557.O7858S87 2001   C813'.6   C2001-900322-6
PR9199.3.D68S87 2001

Canadä   The Canada Council | Le Conseil des Arts
           for the Arts | du Canada

We acknowledge the financial support of the Government of Canada through the Book Publishing Industry Development Program (BPIDP) and the Canada Council for our publishing activities.

For my whole family

I know that night is not the same as day: that all things are different, that the things of the night cannot be explained in the day, because they do not then exist, and the night can be a dreadful time for lonely people once their loneliness had started. But with Catherine there was almost no difference in the night except that it was an even better time. If people bring so much courage to this world the world has to kill them to break them, so of course it kills them. The world kills everyone and afterward many are strong at the broken places. But those that will not break it kills. It kills the very good and the very gentle and the very brave impartially. If you are none of these you can be sure it will kill you too but there will be no special hurry.

Ernest Hemingway
For Whom The Bell Tolls

CHapteR 1

A cursed rain was falling. The phone was cold on her ear, and a solid draft was coming in under the door. What a spot! thought Freda MacDougall at the entrance to her hotel. She was dialing her friend's number at the public telephone.

"My God, Wilena, it's good to hear your voice. I'm at this place called the Granite Arch, on Richards Street. I got here Tuesday and meant to call you right away, but I'm only now finding where the pay phone is. It's outside the lobby, right alongside a Chinese restaurant, where one of them is inside staring right out at me as we speak."

"You mean like when I went up your way and everyone was staring at me?"

"Yes, but that time was because of ugliness."

Both women laughed good-naturedly into the phone and were happy to be talking again.

"Well, how the hell did you get over there?" said Wilena. "Nice part of town to be in."

"Don't I know it's a nice part of town! Ah, someone pointed me here when I got off the bus."

"Well, point yourself right over this way then. I'll get Bobby to come and pick you up. You remember Bobby."

"No, Wilena, I'll come there in a taxi. You don't have to..."

"Shut up. He's right here, and if he can't do that little bit for his mother, well...Let me ask him....Freda? You still there? Yes, he'll need an hour. He'll be there at five. You be downstairs waiting, okay, at five? Hang on...The Granite Arch. He knows it."

Freda said goodbye and hung up the phone. She looked at the Chinese man working inside the restaurant and he stared back. That's just their way, she told herself, going back inside the lobby.

This was Freda's second day in Vancouver, but she felt as if she had been here years. The hotel and its people had all become too familiar too fast. This elevator, for example, with its cranky old motor and narrow doors, was a big part of her day now, and she knew it. The stupid thing took forever to come when you pressed the button, and there were only seven floors. Most aggravating of all was the scrutiny that came from Reception. The workers there eyeballed Freda's every move, especially when she had to stand and wait for the elevator. Theirs were the first faces she had to look at in the morning and the last ones to see at night. Initially, she had been nice to them, till she learned they were watching her comings and goings with their brazen eyes. Coming in was the worst; at least when you were leaving you could get out quickly.

The big peppermint lights above the doors showed that the elevator was now stopped on the fifth floor. Must be the drunks up there, Freda said to herself. The place is crawling with them. Them and cockroaches. She shuddered, then turned a little to where she could covertly glimpse Reception. Madge, the woman clerk, was on. The other two—Lance, the soft pasty one who spoke through his nose, and Bruce, the rail-thin non-smoker with the macho-man's moustache—had the night and early morning shifts respectively. Madge had her head down, pretending to be reading a newspaper. Freda could see where her hair was burnt right to the scalp with bleach. A terrifying part came down over the top of her head, and a pair of glasses covered most of her gnarled beak.

Earlier in the day, Freda had gone to ask about staying two weeks instead of the one week first agreed upon. The creature looked at Freda and contorted her face before agreeing to check Freda in for longer.

The elevator arrived, and the doors opened. The three Bosnian cleaning ladies stood inside. Each, with the dimensions of sturdy bookshelves, held still a moment; they were finished for the day and had on their street clothes. Freda had run into them a few times already. All three had brown bally eyes which looked ready to burst, especially when they were focusing on understanding what was being said to them. There was a war in their country and Freda had been following it back in Cape Breton. The thing was too complicated for her to comprehend, however. She told them this, and it relaxed their eyes some, but she was unsure then whether she had said the right thing. Each had a vinyl purse tucked under a breast and a bus ticket in hand.

"Yas're finished for the day, are yas?" said Freda.

They all looked at her, at first saying nothing. Then, "Yes, yes. Finished, finished. Bye, bye."

They liked that, speaking all at once, and repeating themselves. Freda let them go and stepped into the elevator. She pressed a knuckle to the button for the third floor and stood in the corner, studying the other buttons on the panel. The button for her floor had been melted, by a cigarette lighter, probably. She looked at the industrial carpet on the floor, grey and peppered with more butt burns. The original carpet no doubt, as old as these burnt buttons and the no-smoking sign on the wall and the brown plastic panelling throughout. As old as the dim light overhead with its collection of dead flies in the shade. The cables better be new though, she thought as the doors closed. The elevator started, begrudgingly taking her up.

Stepping out on the third floor, she was confronted by the usual sickening smell of cockroach powder and burnt marijuana. She had no idea what the stink was till a floor resident, the bearded Bible-quoter, explained it to her yesterday. He had been going on about some religious foolishness in the elevator, so Freda asked about the smell just to shut him up. Her mistake was talking to him in the first place, she soon found out, but she had wanted to know where the library was. He looked normal enough, but she remembered how strange he was when he answered.

"It's the library you want," had been his first words. "Oh, of course, that would be the Roman-style cola-see-um library, wouldn't it?"

"I guess so. The new one."

"Yes, well, I don't like Romans as a matter of fact."

"Oh..."

"Yes, they put to death my Saviour. And I, in fact, know what I say to be true as I have had the devil on my back. Twice." He showed her where. "It's true—twice. He was clinging to me, literally, twice. First was when I was a soldier, and I was in the throes of war..." He stopped speaking here, and shut his eyes. Freda stood still, focused on the panelling, the floor, the buttons, and the dead flies, listening for the gears.

"Very well, very well," his whiskered mouth began again. "There I was on my back, which had been literally snapped in two. Literally, two halves, when the Lord spoke to me directly for the first time." He then reached in his coat pocket and took out a Bible. The elevator was stopped, and Freda was out in the hallway with him, looking into the small red book, its pages new and hardly cracked. He began reading a psalm, his voice ringing queerly out into the dim hall with its shut doors up and down either side. Freda was a Catholic, a Roman one at that, but she didn't care for this man's religion. Religion belongs in a church, she had wanted to tell him. Besides, there was liquor on his breath.

"What's that smell out here?" She turned her nose down the hall. His face shot up and he answered decisively, "One part roach powder, two parts dope." Freda was at her room before he had a chance to return to the subject at hand. He called out to her, inviting her to some Bible and doughnut night that was going on somewhere. She was busy with her son, she told him, then went inside her room.

What a queer bird that was, she thought now, definitely someone to stay away from. Vancouver....If anyone wants to know the truth, it's hateful, and no place to be at all. Frustrating, everything distorted, foreign, and miserable.

*

Freda had forty-five minutes before Bobby came. Her room had a big window that looked down over the crossroads of Richards and West Pender. The light was now low there. A woman not much younger than Freda stood in the street below, her hair dyed, and over her shoulders a cheap slutty jacket with mangy yellow material all around the collar. She was approaching people going past. At first, Freda couldn't figure out what she was after, but then one young man in a blue hard-hat stopped, reached in his pocket, and put money in her hand. A beggar, then. The jacket must be a holdover from a time when she had something worth selling. Freda could hardly believe where she was, in a miserable Vancouver hotel, a filthy, dirty, drug-ridden hotel with city prostitutes and city slackards, and thieves on every corner. You be solid as a rock, she told herself looking now in the mirror of her hotel room. Keep solid as a rock. You can take anything they dish out here, and always have. In your whole sixty-four years, you have. Your hair might be grey, but it's not dry since you decided to stop with that shampoo. Your eyes are still a clear hazel, eyelashes nice and long yet. Your chin is sharp, and can be counted on for a long time more. There are wrinkles now, but better than when they first started to appear. The lips are full, too; they have not betrayed anyone. They look good even before they are made up, and that little scar in the upper one—taken from a dog as a child—has not changed at all since first healing. It has always enhanced my looks, she thought. But isn't that funny, no one ever asks me about it, but it is the first thing I notice when I look at my own face.

Drawing her shoulders back and touching her breasts, she said aloud, "Yes, solid as the red rocks of Smokey." The big bold rocks that stand out over the sea in Ingonish and have for generations, prompting contemplation of the many lives that passed below, the aging of a community, the dotage of one, where only a few grains were ever tossed down to the tides below. Oh, dear Jesus, thought Freda, take me home. Take me home now, I don't want to be here another second. Come for me, someone. But no one can now, now that they all know I've left—that they all know I am here. But it's so miserable out here, hateful. Nothing is natural or with any sense. You were the one who wanted to come, she told herself, drawing her shoulders back again.

"Wisen up, you're stronger than this," she said into the mirror but didn't mean it and turned herself away.

*

It was getting late and Freda had only fifteen minutes left to get ready. She heaved her suitcase up onto the bed, opened it and looked at the clothes she had brought. The grey slacks and blue sweater would do. It was definitely a warmer climate out here, but there was still the chill of back home in her bones. Freda had brought a pair of pantyhose and knew that they would help some. Stripping off and bending over to step into them, she lost her balance.

"Cursed old frig," she said. "These damn things." She sat on the bed and worked them up. Her sisters, Emma and Wanda, had shown her as a child how to roll them first, then put them on, but she had never managed to make a good roll and always ended by yanking them on in a sloppy way. Christ almighty, I'm going to rip them, she thought. I should have brought leotards, they're always easy. The thin brown material seemed to disappear as she brought it up over her navel, snapping the elastic waist.

"There," she said, her voice sounding odd against the plastered walls. When she was dressed she put on her coat and picked up her purse, remembering to check for her wallet and also to lock the door.

In the lobby she nodded toward the front desk, but her proffered greeting was ignored, as usual. Madge was still on, her newspaper open and a cigarette burning away in the hand that was holding the paper. If only she would ignite, thought Freda, while making her way past the bleached creature. The cigarette would light the paper, and the paper would light the woman. She would surely burn for weeks with all the alcohol in her; she knew a drinker when she saw one.

Outside it was mild, and a breeze was swirling overhead. Standing alongside the hotel and watching people go by, Freda made up her mind that no one here was fit to look at. Hair hung off the men; the girls' heads were shaved as if they had been diagnosed with lice. Sickening, all of it. If only they would ask me what I thought of them, oh, what a railing I'd give! How in God's good name do they expect to be looked at favourably when they parade around in public like that?

She looked across the street to pacify herself. The woman she had seen asking for money was no longer begging. A black man in a little chocolate Datsun drove up. He rolled down his window a little and craned his neck to call out: "You Freda?"

"So far." She walked toward the car, grinning. The man got out; he was a good six feet tall. His smile revealed an even set of teeth, and nothing in the world is better than a good set of teeth.

"I'm Bobby, Freda."

"Hello, Bobby-Freda."

"Oh, a sense of humour, I like that. Didn't keep you waiting, did I?"

"No, I was just admiring the street life." She tried to open the car door.

"Wait, that's a little tricky." He came over to show Freda how to squeeze, not lift, the handle. The cars going by were noisy, and Freda had a job listening to his lovely instructions. Bobby was slow and generous with words, the sound of his voice low and helpful like a priest's. She thanked him, and once inside the car, she took the seat belt and drew it across her front. Bobby had gone around and was easing his body in through the driver's little door.

"Don't bother with the belts. There's plenty of them, but they don't work. You're just going to have to trust me."

As he eased them into the traffic of Richards Street, Freda spied the beggar woman eating a tremendous slice of pizza. Freda waited for Bobby to speak, but he was concentrating.

"How's about if I tie them around me and knot them?"

"What's that?"

"The seat belts."

Again, the teeth.

"You could, but I don't know if the material would hold you." Checking his rear-view mirror and then over his shoulder, he switched lanes. He was a good driver. The Datsun bucked a few times before doing what he wanted it to do. Once it got going, though, the little car began to keep up with the rest of them.

"What year is she?"

"Who, Mom?"

"No, I know she's ancient. The car."

"She's a '74, and all mine." They burst out laughing and had trouble stopping, especially Freda. Oh, it was good to be with people again.

The car paused in traffic under a big red light suspended by cables and bounced above the intersection. Freda observed how the faces in the cars seemed to come from every corner of the earth: Chinese, Indian, Mexican. Freda looked at Bobby's face.

"Been out here a while?" she said.

"Let's see…" The big light overhead turned green, and the car bounced out into the intersection. "I left home in the spring of '79. That must make it seventeen years. That's right, this spring will be my seventeenth. Whew, that's a while, eh? But it's good out here, a lot's going on." Bobby looked over at Freda and widened his eyes in a happy way. She noticed his receding hairline, especially at his temples. His hair was short all over, made up of tiny, pretty curls which looked like a little field of iron filings or a wooly helmet.

They spun around a corner, and Freda heard a quick, loud grinding noise from the car's rear axle.

"Not to worry, dear. My springs are bad back there. But only in the right turns does she act up. Otherwise, she purrs like a kitten. I'm going to get a block of wood under her this weekend. See if I can't prop up the old dear, so to speak. What we got to do to preserve history, eh, Freda?"

"Yeah, what we got to do."

I like this fellow, she thought. He's easy to be with right away, and that's just what the doctor ordered. He's big, too, and a bit of security never hurt a woman. Then again, here we are rolling down the highway in busy traffic in a twenty-two-year-old Datsun with a door handle you have to squeeze to open, seat belts that don't work, rear tires scraping against the body. Where's the security in any of that? But it was there, somehow. It was there.

Freda smiled warmly at her thoughts, then realized she had been smiling since she got in the car.

"You'll have to answer this a lot, Freda, but how do you like Vancouver? Little different for you out here, I imagine."

"Different, yes. But it's like anything, it has to grow on you. To tell you the truth, Bobby, I haven't seen any of it yet. It's only been two days since I got here, and the first of that was spent getting straightened away. Yesterday, I got a chance to walk a spell. I went around that Air Canada Place, or Canada Place, rather, in the morning. Quite a show down there, I'll tell you. All kinds of trains bringing people in, taking them right back out. Helicopters and little harbour planes at the same job, leaving the water like dragonflies. The whole bay was like a garden full of bugs on the first warm day of summer. What a commotion."

"Right on, you're seeing it."

"Yes, I am, and she's a busy spot all right. But the mountains, now, they're really the thing out here. The size, and the snow on them!"

"Well that's just where I happen to be going tonight. A few of us go to this place called Grouse Mountain every Thursday after work, for a hike. It only takes about an hour to get up, but it's a workout. There's an overhead tram we ride back down. Let's see, there's Tom—another Maritimer. Gilles is from Montreal. Pat, a local fella, born and raised here, the only one I know who is. And, oh yes, Adrien, who sometimes comes. He might be from Montreal, too, I'm not so sure. They're a great group of fellas. I'll introduce you to them. They're a good bunch to know out here."

What is this? thought Freda. He likes to go on about people I haven't met and wouldn't know from a hole in the wall. This is what a child does, expecting you to know all about their friends right away, after saying their names.

"We're right here on the left. Listen Freda. I've been after Mom to come over with us some evening, not to climb of course, but to take the tram up. Now that you're out here, you could both come along. It's well worth seeing."

"Are you sure there's no climbing?"

"Na, not a bit. The bus lets you off at the station and you take the lift from there straight up to a chalet at the top. It's easy but trying to coax Mom to go anywhere is like trying to persuade a train off its track. Talk to her will ya, get her to come. Both of you. There's no need of her sitting around the apartment all day with Norman and smoking cigarettes."

"Norman?"

"Her cat."

Bobby pulled the Datsun into a small driveway that angled down under an apartment building to a garage door. He rolled down his window and inserted a key into a lock in the concrete wall. The garage door opened with a long groan.

"Nifty," said Freda.

"Yeah, you don't even have to get out. Pretty soon we won't have to get up out of our chairs. Life will be lived without ever having to straighten up."

He drove underground and wheeled into a tiny space set off by white lines. The parking lot was dim and damp, and the ceiling was very low. Good place to be murdered, thought Freda, who was looking over at Bobby in the darkness. She noticed a dripping sound, and the smell of cat piss.

"Think about that climb, Freda. Promise me now. It will get you up in those mountains."

"I will."

Bobby had to frig with the car locks before he got them to open. The two walked across wet pavement to a grey steel door that was set in the concrete wall. Bobby held it open for Freda and she brushed past him. The door looked awfully heavy.

"This big thing keeps all the burglars out," said Bobby. "I've had my car broken into four times."

"Why?"

"What do you mean, *why*? You think my car's a beater? It's a good car, come on now. Usually they just rifle through the dash on the lookout for money, but a window is usually broken in the process. Consider yourself lucky, Freda, you came at a good time. You got a ride without taped-up windows."

They rode a small modern elevator. They stood quietly.

Ah, I am about to see Wilena, thought Freda. Better get some wisecracks ready. But wisecracks aren't something you can get ready for, with her. Wilena was one person who could match Freda when she got going. Wilena's mouth was fast and deliberate, sometimes harsh. But that, among other things, was what drew them together. They were instantly comfortable with each other. Yes, thought Freda, saying Wilena is direct comes a little short of the mark.

The elevator was bright; mirrors were on every wall. Freda and Bobby held their gaze steady on the elevator doors, as if expecting gunmen to burst in. But when the doors opened there were no gunmen, just a great length of plush carpet running down a hallway.

"When was the last time you saw Mom?"

"It's been a while." They navigated short hallways and passed through more doors—fire doors, Bobby explained. The halls were narrower here and the ceilings lower than in the hotel. Architects had their way in this place, thought Freda, and people got the short end of the stick. Tomb-like parking, electric doors, fire doors, theft doors, mirrored elevators, skinny hallways. You had safety, sure, she thought; efficiency and privacy, too, but what was most important had been bartered away: space and simplicity. They went through the last fire door.

"Here we are," said Bobby. "Right down here, 404. I live back the other way, in 414. Same floor and, oh, how convenient it is, living on the same floor as your mother!" He winked and Freda grinned. "We're okay, though, as long as we stay out of each other's hair."

"Not much fear of anyone getting into yours."

"Jesus! We hardly just met each other and you're going on about my hair. I'm sensitive about that, you know. Doesn't matter, a receding hairline is a sign of wisdom."

"I thought that racket coming down the hallway was trouble," came another voice.

Wilena. She stood in the doorway of her apartment, an arm stretched up against the casing. She wore the same foggy glasses as always, and was trying to hide a burning cigarette behind her.

"She giving you a hard time, Bob? Didn't try to get you into a bar, did she? Nothing but pure devil this one."

The women laughed, hugging each other.

"I'll let you two get at your lies," said Bobby. "I've got to go meet the guys."

"Yes, you go and meet the guys," said Wilena with odd intonation.

"Shut up, Mom. I'm already late. Now don't go talking about me when I'm gone, you hear me, Ma? I'll give you a lift to the hotel when I get back, Freda."

"Ah, don't bother, Bobby. I can get a taxi."

He lifted his arm and waved off the idea as he headed down the hall. Freda called out to thank him, and he waved again.

"Good fella, that," said Freda.

*

"She ain't much to look at, but she's got a door that keeps the wolves way," said Wilena inside the apartment. "And by Christ if thur ain't a lot of them around here. Sit, sit."

"What do you mean? The bums, is it?" said Freda removing her shoes and lining them up neatly on a transparent welcome mat.

"Yes, for Christ's sake. Bums, hookers, thieves, bandits, you name it. They're a hard bunch out here, I'm telling ya. You got to watch your back. But I shouldn't say that stuff. It's not so bad once you get used to it."

"I've seen quite the sights myself already over at Richards Street, where the hotel is."

"Now, let's not knock the place too much."

"You started it! You haven't changed, Wilena."

"Richards Street. That's the threshold to it all right there, that East Side. I'll tell you here and now, I wouldn't set foot in that area supposing the sun was high in the sky! Drugs and dope is all that place is! We're going to have to move you out of there, love, and do it today, before we have you staggering around look- ing for more pills or something." Standing in the middle of the living room, Wilena held the hand with the cigarette in it to her lips and stretched out her neck to take a drag. She smiled and sat in a tea-coloured rocking chair, beside which was a large glass ashtray containing two butts that had been smoked right down to the filter.

"How are you getting along, without him, I mean? It must be hard, dear, hard as hell." Wilena extinguished her cigarette and exhaled lightly, then blew out the rest of the smoke from deep in her lungs. She started to rock in her chair. "It was hard on me when Austin finally went his merry way. But you know all that now, I imagine. We go ahead, but you know that, too, eh. We go ahead, and you can only take so much of that thinking business. That's what drives you batty—it's what'll finish you off entirely, too. After a while, when you're ready of course, a person settles down. When you finally get tired of all that thinking, then you can get some rest. But I know it's not all that long, and you and Milty were always together. You'll beat it, I know that for a fact, you made it all the way out here. So did I. He never did take a drink, did he?"

Freda shifted her weight on the little chesterfield, which was hard and low and not at all comfortable.

"No, he was always good that way. Perhaps he should have from time to time. No, he was good that way. The only thing that really stays with me now is how tired he got toward the end. People say they're tired, they say it all the time. Well, here's one who knows now what tired is. I lived with it the whole last year he was alive... The other thing was how quiet he got—there was such a change in him. He wouldn't say a word and neither would I, for a time. No one did, not about what was happening. But he got through that part then started talking about how the Lord didn't want him and was turning him away. I thought that was just part of the foolishness he always went on with. You know how he was."

"I do."

"I could tell, though, that he believed in some of his foolishness. Long before, when he couldn't get around, when he couldn't do work around the house no more—it was then that he started saying those things about the hearse when it would be bringing someone's remains down for a funeral in Ingonish. He'd look out the window and say he was going down and get a few steaks off the body for supper. Awful stuff, I know, but he'd say it. At first, I would laugh if someone was in, just to go along with him. I'd call out and say what an awful tongue he had. I'd say he was going right to the belly of hell if he kept it up. He'd just continue, though, saying how tender the cuts would be especially if so and so was a good Catholic. Oh, the stuff he went on with. I could tell, though, towards the end when he got quiet, when I knew it was going to take him, I could tell that he was flesh and bones like the rest of us. He knew that, too. Everyone knows soon enough. The tired part and the quiet part, that's what got to me most. I didn't care for that one bit."

"I know all about it, dear." Wilena leaned ahead in her chair and looked at Freda, bringing comfort. "But enough of this moaning. Let's get a good old-fashioned cup of tea going. Get up off your arse and come help me in the kitchen. Or no, wait, you'll be in my way. Just stay there while I make it."

Wilena straightened up out of her rocking chair and left. Freda watched the empty chair move on its own. From the kitchen, Wilena called back, "Been up to Richmond Hall, lately? Before you come out, I mean? Do I ever miss the old gang there, but I plan to go back for a visit this summer. That is, if the good Lord himself doesn't drop by to collect me to play in his own hall by then."

"That frigging game!" Freda sang out. "Don't get me going! I was up to Sydney with Gloria a few weeks back and for the first time in years I was set for the jackpot. It was twenty-five hundred that night. I was set on two cards. Four calls came up—four now!—and do you think my number was any one of them? Cursed old frig, a B-4 was all I needed, a raggedly old B-4! They're probably calling it out right now in every hall across the country. I swore inside and out, driving back down to Ingonish, that I was through, I was giving it up for good. Foolishness is what it is."

Wilena was moving around in the kitchen, and Freda could hear the kettle starting to heat. It sounded full.

"What! Go home, girl! Every time I see you, you go on like this. But come a good old-fashioned game somewhere, and you're the first outside the hall waiting to get in, lining up to get your cards like any of the rest of us."

"It's the only thing a person's got in this day and age, Wilena. You know that same as me."

Freda could hear the cupboards banging. "What are you doing out there? I hope you're not going through any trouble." She rose and went to the kitchen. The kettle was beginning to growl, and there was a porcelain teapot, the same colour as the rocking chair in the living room, set out.

"Here, sit down here," said Wilena pulling a chair out from a kitchen table that was too big for the room. "I'm preparing a snack."

"A cup of tea is enough. Come on now, Wilena."

"What? And waste away to nothing? We need to be fortified, girl, always. Sit down, Ranald." Wilena liked to call Freda by the old-time names. She had learned the practice while on a visit to Ingonish years ago. She had thought it immediately hilarious when she heard people doing it.

"Just don't go to any trouble."

"Trouble? That's all you've ever been."

Freda sat and, despite feeling her legs confined under the table, she much preferred the kitchen because it was brighter and warmer. Wilena set down a plate of Oreos in the centre of the table. Wilena wasn't much for cooking, Freda knew; she herself had admitted this. Most of her meals came from a can, but that was her way and it was fine. Just then something brushed against Freda's slacks. Looking down she saw an enormous cat, its belly fat beyond measure.

"What the hell is it?"

"What?"

"What's wrong with it?"

"What, what!"

"The cat. Here, puss, puss."

"Oh, I thought you found a big spider or something."

Freda put her hand down. The cat looked up at her lazily and then seemed to decide that touching the hand was too much work. It waddled back under the table.

"For frig sakes, Wilena, are you trying to murder the poor thing? She's as big as a house!" Freda could smell the litter box now and was sure it was somewhere in the kitchen. Some of the cat hair had stuck to her slacks and reaching down to pick it off, she saw more of it rise in the air and land on her sweater. She noticed that she had also picked up a good deal from the chesterfield in the living room. She turned in the chair and looked down.

"Don't be so foolish," said Wilena. "He just needs a little exercise is all. Don't you, Norman? In the summer me and him are going back home for a trip to New Waterford, and he's going to catch one of those big black crows that fly over the pier. Aren't you, fella?"

Wilena placed two good cups and saucers on the table, then brought the teapot in.

"Norman?" said Freda. "Pretty name for a cat. You'll give the thing a complex."

"I'll give you a complex, right above where I land this cup. It's a good name, a sensible name. It don't matter what something's called anyway. You grow into your name, same as with people. Doesn't matter what you get."

"I suppose." Freda held her cup for some tea. Wilena poured, then she served herself before sliding a cribbage board out from below a big stack of letters. She dug through the same pile and gathered a deck of cards. Freda stirred in the evaporated milk that Wilena had served with the tea. She had cleaned off the top of the milk can, but there was still dried yellow milk caked on one of the holes she had made with a knife.

Wilena was counting out the cards to make sure they were all there. They were a tartan red and their corners were worn, some were bent. She dealt six cards apiece, and each woman took a cookie.

"Hard to get a good game of crib going out here, I imagine," said Freda.

"You got that right. Bobby is the only one I know who plays, and he ain't the swiftest wolf in the pack. He's a fruit, did I tell you?"

"A what?"

"A fruit. You know, he goes the other way. Gay, they call it. Queer."

"Go on!"

"It's true. Damn near tore me apart when I first found out, which was just this past fall, just after I come out. For a spell there I wouldn't talk to him, but how long can that last? He was the only one I had to help me get set up in the apartment. At first, I was going to go straight back to Cape Breton. Something like that is not easy for a mother to take."

Both women sipped their tea cautiously; it was still very hot.

"No, I don't imagine it is easy," said Freda. "All I know, Wilena, is that he seems like gold to me. Coming over to pick me up like that and talking in the car to make me feel comfortable. He's as much a gentleman as ever any of the old fellows were."

The game had begun, and the small plastic pegs moved up the first stretch of the board.

"Hold on a sec," said Wilena, who went to the living room. Freda heard the TV come on.

"I got to hear today's highlights of the trial," Wilena hollered back. "They put the highlights on every day at six. That's when you get the new stuff, the rest of the day is just repeats. We'll stay in there, though." She returned to the kitchen and took her seat at the table but continued in a loud voice. "Are you following it?"

"Quit screeching, I'm right here. No, not much."

"Well, he's as guilty as sin, and he knows it, too. He'll go for a good ride, the miserable bastard. I'm just watching and waiting for the day they put him away. I want to see his face, that same one that's been wearing this, 'Who, me?' expression for the past ten months."

The two women got back to their game. Freda laid down some nice hands and gained a big lead on Wilena. A panel was discussing the trial on the TV in the other room, but Freda and Wilena didn't bother with it. Freda soon won, and Wilena handed her the cards to deal a new game. "Cheating is the only way you'll win," she said.

"What are you talking about?"

"Never mind it. Yes, Bobby, it nearly killed me. Well, not really. It's like anything else, there's nothing so big that you can't get past it in a few days. Nothing. There's regular life to get on with, groceries to buy, bills to pay. You still have to get up in the morning and put your drawers on before your pants. I let him have it at first, though. I took a strip out of him and told him off black and blue. But what's the good of that? Scream all you want, holler all you want. What could I say, Freda? He never hurt no one in his life, and if that is the life you're living then there's a good bit right about it. The reason he left his home and all his people in the first place was all my doing. He couldn't stay around there with the way things were because what killed him most was how the whole thing would affect me. All those years of never telling me, then, my coming all the way out here and only then does he say something. I must come across as mean sometimes. I am a good person, though, I *try* to be a good person. And you know what? At first, all I could worry about was myself. I worried about holding my head up in public when I went home. We're the old school, Freda. You know that—bingo, church, the people down there. But one night when I was speaking my peace about it, I realized before finishing the rant just who I was. A little old black woman with bad eyes, that's who. Nothing more. Someone who quit smoking seven years ago, and has since then never smoked so much. But that's all anyone is, Freda, just one or two things....It made me climb down off my high horse. I can't change the world, Freda, no one can. And as soon as a person realizes this is when, strangely, things do change. Leave it all alone, don't frig with it, and that's when the peace comes." She pushed her well-worn glasses up on the bridge of her nose, and the cards began to move again. "What about you, Freda?"

"I'm not gay."

"Shut up! You're the tough one, I mean, coming all the way out here—by yourself. What I don't understand, though, is why you didn't come here from the airport and stay with me right off. I know you like to do things your way, you always have, but we're friends."

"I don't like to put people out."

Norman waddled out from under the table and headed for the sink, catching the women's attention.

"For the love of God, Wilena! Put it on a diet so a person can stand to look at it!"

Wilena tried to bend from her chair to reach the cat, but she herself was too fat to do it.

After a few more games of cribbage and more tea, Freda and Wilena moved back into the living room to watch the final hour of the trial highlights. Normally, Freda hated to watch TV when she was visiting someone; but after a few minutes of sitting with Wilena, she enjoyed the show. Wilena got up to take her glass ashtray to the kitchen. "I'm going to wash it," she said, but Freda could smell the tobacco burning while the water was running in the sink.

"For God sakes, Wilena. If you want to smoke, smoke!" But Freda couldn't be heard over the water.

The evening passed quickly and at nine Bobby arrived wearing a pair of hiking boots and long shorts. He stood in the entrance and wouldn't come in, saying he was done out and too tired to bend over to take his boots off. His thick socks that came up just below his knees were full of mud.

"Have a good evening, girls?" he said. "Been talking about me?"

"Freda's been telling me what kind of gentleman you are and how she'd like to have your children. Fine with me, I told her."

Freda looked at Bobby and shook her head. "Was it a good hike? No broken bones I hope?"

"Nope, no trouble at all. Got up in forty-three minutes tonight, a personal best for me. The other guys did well, too. Tom, of course, was the first up. You two catch up on all the gossip?"

"Yes, but the night got better after your mother quit cheating at crib."

"Me? What do I need to cheat for, when there's no one here who can beat me!"

"I beat ya."

"Whenever you're ready to go, Freda?" said Bobby. "Just give me a shout. I'm just going down the hall to change."

"I told her to stay here with me, but she won't listen to sense. She's bent on staying at that hotel when a friend is offering to put her up. We'll have to get her out of there, Bobby."

The cat brushed up against Freda's slacks, and more scraggly hairs stuck.

"I'm all right there. The location is good, the price is right. I'm pretty well right down on Robson Street too, the main drag, I understand."

"All roads here lead to Robson," said Wilena.

"Okay, when you two finish, give me a call."

"I'll bring her down," said Wilena.

After a few minutes the women went out into hall, and Norman followed along. The old friends hugged at Bobby's door, and Freda promised she would call first thing in the morning. Wilena called out to the cat, then went after it. She had little difficulty catching him, he was moving so slowly. Freda watched Wilena struggle with the heavy cat in her arms as she took it back to her apartment.

cHapteR 2

In the car on the way back to the hotel, Bobby asked about Ingonish. Freda found herself filled with talk about life there. She told him about the beauty, the characters, and about how peaceful it was. "You might never get ahead there," she said. "But you never get behind." She felt homesick and felt sorry that she was going back to her hotel to be alone. But it's only been two days, she reminded herself, then fell quiet in the car.

She thought of her Aunt Bridget, who used to take the Mount Cabot bus up to Sydney. Aunt Bridget would go out to the road in the early morning to wait for the bus. It would be late spring, and Freda, just a girl then, would be playing with her sister and brothers in the ditches or the puddles when she'd see her aunt leave. The trip took two hours if there weren't many passengers to pick up along the north shore. Bridget would stay in Sydney for two days at a time, which seemed like a stretch back then, but what struck Freda now was how changed her aunt would be by the time she returned from one of these trips. Stepping down off the bus in the evening, she would first look around, then walk deferentially up to the house. She would call out to the kids in an altered accent, hold her head up in a new way for a response. These short trips changed her whole person. It was as if she had gained from her travels some kind of immediate sophistication, a shift in culture, an elevation of some sort. "How are you, Freda?" she would call out dramatically going down to the house. "It's so nice to see you!" she would say and then, of course, "How you've grown, Freda!" The kids would squeal at this; they would call out and make fun of her, but she would continue to walk into the house with her shoulders back, head high, offering her profile only and smiling at their little ribalds.

Freda understood Aunt Bridget and her trips, now, in a tiny Datsun in Vancouver, on a midwinter night more than fifty years later. Had she become like her aunt? The little car deposited her outside the hotel and spun itself back out into the traffic again before the answer came. Rain dripped a long way off the hotel roof. She remembered the trip on the airplane that brought her here. It was a good trip, she thought, and a smile came across her face when she pictured Jimmy taking her to the airport.

*

Jimmy was not nervous by nature, but behind the wheel he was and always drove with both hands planted firmly at ten and two, eyes straight ahead. In winter it was awful to have to drive with him, but there was no longer any bus service, so it was the only way to get to the airport. They left in the dark. Freda said a couple of Hail Marys going down over Cape Smokey, but silently so as not to bother Jimmy, who was concentrating. It was frosty, and the roads along the north shore were covered with ice. Just before Skir Dhu a big deer jumped out from the trees, and Jimmy saw it only after it was across his lane. Jamming on the brakes, he sent them into a skid first then turned them completely around in the middle of the road.

"For frig sakes, Jimmy!" said Freda, a little too harshly.

"Take her easy, dear. I'll get us there," he said, shimmying the wheel, getting his hands back in place. They drove on in a heavier silence, but when they came to the straight stretch at Piper's the sun was up and it broke through to brighten the road ahead. From there the roads were good, straight through to Sydney. They were at the airport an hour and a half early. Freda tried to give Jimmy ten dollars for gas—he had decided to leave because it was starting to snow again—but he shook his head at the money.

"Go on now, don't go showing me that," he said. "You'll need it out there."

"Smarten up, Jimmy, you got us up here in the dark of winter. I appreciate it, so take it."

"I know you appreciate it, Freda, but I don't want to be taking money from you."

"Come on, you and Gloria have the new baby coming. Take it."

Jimmy reached two fingers out of the crack at the top of the car window, and Freda creased the bill better to pass it in. Jimmy pressed in on the clutch and brake as they exchanged final farewells. He put the car in gear, making the ash from his cigarette fall onto the rubber casing of the gearshift. A tiny swirl of blue smoke puffed from the car's tailpipe, and the tires crunched the knotty ice of the airport parking lot. Then he was gone.

Freda was left holding her suitcase, standing in her bright green winter coat in the falling snow.

She went into the airport to look for the departure desk. There was a small lineup at the check-in counter. When Freda's turn came a woman asked for her ticket and whether she needed any bags checked.

"The only bag I need checked is me," she said. But there was no response; the woman was all business. Allowed to keep her suitcase with her, Freda was instructed to follow a little group out to the runway. One fellow in the group wore his hair long, but he had a neatly clipped beard. He was carrying a guitar with stickers on it and looked to be a little scared. Freda smiled good-naturedly at him.

"I hope you're going to give us a tune on board," she said over to him, but he only smiled back and twisted his head a little. Can't be much of a performer, she thought, shy like that.

They soon boarded the aircraft and Freda found her seat; it was small but had good padding. Hardly anyone was on board—perhaps because it was still early—but Freda couldn't imagine them bothering to take off with so few. The guy with the guitar was sitting all by himself, too, at the front. His heavy winter jacket puffed up high over the shoulders and made him look silly, as if it were his first time anywhere. Freda thought of going to talk to him but was afraid to leave her seat, now that she was in it. She studied her seat belt instead, then clipped it on. The thing was the same as what they had in the old cars, just a strong straight strap tightened at the hips. Pulling it taut, she looked up at the husky musician again. He could be carrying the guitar for someone else, maybe.

The plane ride from Sydney to Halifax was short; the plane seemed to go up only to come straight back down. Freda had stared out her window the whole way, especially as they were moving over Cape Breton. Her sixty-four years were spent down there somewhere, and seemed to have gone by just as quickly as this flight. Simple from here, easy and quick from here, she thought.

Upon landing in Halifax, the stewardess told the passengers to transfer. Walking from the plane through a cold chute that stretched out from the airport like a giant arm, Freda felt as if she were going from winter into summer. It was mild and bright inside the airport, but most impressive was the number of people—some sitting, some standing, others going here and there, some dressed in T-shirts. And the size of it all! It looked like a big shopping mall with wide, wide corridors. Everyone had luggage on trolleys. The faces she saw were from all over the world, thought Freda, noticing turbans and dark skin. Back home in Ingonish, she'd be lucky to find the road ploughed, and not one car would be out. She kept looking around. So this is what I am now, a flyer, a traveller.

She had some time before her next plane left. With suitcase in hand, she followed the signs for the cafeteria and made her way down to have a look at what they had to eat. As it was early in the day yet, many people were eating their breakfast. She walked along the glass display case to check the prices. Christ almightly, the prices they're charging! A bowl of cereal is scandalous—I could buy two whole boxes of porridge for that, she thought. Everything's scandalous! What can I afford here? Maybe a package of salt, a thing or two of ketchup. Cutthroats! she thought. But there's the one thing always to watch, she told herself: money.

She poured a small cup of orange juice, and took it to the counter. She held her breath as the woman rang up the total, then added the tax. It came to almost two dollars! Mercy me, I'll be broke before I get out of the province. She found a seat and drank the juice, which tasted like hell and was made from some cheap crystal substitute. After two sips more she decided just to sit and wait, but there was no one to look at here. She got up and went to find the gate for her next plane.

She had to wait in line to pass through security before she could get to the gates. The people here were silent and guilty looking. When it came her turn Freda, who had been watching, knew what to do. Heaving her suitcase up on a conveyor belt, she let it pass through an X-ray machine. A black man with a sloping chest told her to walk forward under a tall arched door frame. When she did, the alarm went off. The man stepped up and asked her to raise her arms. He began waving a pink stick up and down her sides.

"If you make me disappear with this stick of yours, don't go collecting my pension cheque, now will ya."

"I won't." The man laughed. He had a proper set of teeth and seemed like a nice fellow.

"You're okay," he said. "Go ahead. I won't touch your cheque, even though I'm sure it's probably twice what mine is." His lips settled to a warm grin, and he told Freda where to take the escalator up to the departure lounge. She was happy that her suitcase had gone through. The main reason she carried it with her was so no one could stash anything illegal in it then say it was hers when she was caught with whatever they were trying to smuggle, drugs probably.

The gate was easy to find. The furniture made it look like a waiting room for a doctor's office, only it was more wide-open. There were some seats facing the wall-size windows, and Freda sat there. The day beyond the glass was grey and wintry but easy on the eyes. Space and more flatness than she had ever seen surrounded the airport. The Prairies must be like this, she thought. I will have to look down when we fly over. Some spruce trees, far off to the right, skinny and starved looking, each had a little flag waving on it. Where the hell are all the planes? she wondered.

"You survived the first leg of the journey."

Freda turned and squinted. It was the guitar fellow.

"Yes, made it this far," she said. He sat down opposite her and leaned his guitar on the seat next to him, but the floor was slippery, and the guitar kept getting away from him.

"Where are you off to today?" Freda asked. He was preoccupied with his guitar and had to stand it straight up on the seat before giving his answer.

"Toronto. Going out to stay with my brother. I was just out there this past fall, but I'm going to stay a while this time. I finished a cooking course before Christmas, and there's supposed to be a bit of work out there right now."

"Oh, I see. That's a good line to be in I imagine, cooking. People need to eat." Freda wanted to tell him her name, but it seemed as if too much time had passed for that. Perhaps people don't like to introduce themselves when they're flying anyway, she thought.

"I'm off to Vancouver," she said. "It's my first time out. That plane we were on back there was the first time I ever got any higher than the ladder up to the attic of my house."

"Suppose! It was last fall for me. Some way to go, isn't it?"

"Yes, it's some machine all right. It's like heading up over the mountains in a mobile home."

The man looked at Freda. "Wally Deagle," he said, and shot out his hand.

"Hi, Wally. I'm Freda MacDougall."

"Pleasure to meet you, Freda."

"A Deagle and a MacDougall, a pair of Scots. Not only the planes, but the lies'll be flying now."

"You got that right. This is quite the trip you're making, Freda, all the way out to Vancouver. And you're all alone, aren't you?"

"For the travelling part, yes. A good friend of mine from New Waterford is out there. She invited me out. I used to go up and play bingo with her in around Sydney when she lived there. We're great friends."

"Used to go up from where?"

"From Ingonish."

"Oh, Ingonish. I knew a fellow from down there. I went to university for a spell with him. Donovan. Said he lived on Main Street."

"Main Street? Oh, there isn't much of a Main Street in Ingonish, I'm afraid. But I think I know who you mean. I just can't remember his name."

"Nice fellow, I can't think of his name either now. I'm from over Inverness way. You must've been over there once or twice."

"Land sakes, yes! I used to go over there all the time with my husband, Milton. We used to go over to the Broad Cove fiddle concerts. The last going off, though, we had to quit it and steer clear. They were all getting right crazy in the field with the liquor and spoiling it for the rest who went there for the music. Don't get me wrong, though, I don't deny a person their drink. No, I'll even allow myself the odd one from time to time, when the occasion is right. It's just when they start getting right foolish on it."

"Yes, well…The fiddle, you say? There's this older player from Cape North. That's down your way, I believe. Ah, what the frig is his name? I seen him up in Halifax a couple of weeks back. He was tearing the roof off the place and coming back on the instrument like he was wringing the neck of an old she-cat. Fitzgerald! That's it. Yes, he put on some show, I'll tell you. Wasn't much of a place to

watch him in, though. Everyone was standing and you couldn't see
a thing, the poor old fella hardly had a chance to breathe."

"Don't go worrying about that. I never heard tell of a fiddle player
yet who didn't have a chance to breed."

Wally let out a smoker's laugh and finished off choking. His teeth
were bad, but he had a nice mouth. Freda laughed along.

An announcement came overhead: "Air Canada flight 45 to Vancouver, with stops in Toronto and Calgary, is now preparing for
departure. Would all those requiring assistance kindly…"

"That's us, Freda," Wally said, standing, hiking up the big jeans
he wore and tucking in his shirt.

He and Freda talked some more while waiting in the lineup for
the gate, but when they got aboard the aircraft they wished each
other luck as their seats were far apart again. Freda's was at the very
back this time, the last row on the plane. This must be where they
put the old women from Cape Breton on the big flights, she thought.
Probably to keep them away from the food carts and the bar. There
is one good thing about it, though, the toilet is right behind.

Jamming her suitcase below at her feet, she sat down. When everyone else was sitting, a stewardess appeared at the front of the aisle
and started a series of instructions explaining what to do should the
plane go down. Good, Freda thought. Encouragement. What the hell
are they trying to do, stop my heart altogether before we go up again?
They didn't do this on the first flight, or did they? The stewardess
was pointing to the exits. She moved her arms in very sincere ges-
tures as she indicated where to go in the event of a disaster.

Freda studied her face. The woman looked to be in her mid-for-
ties, and unmarried. Yes, unmarried; she is looking around too much
for someone who is married, thought Freda. Maybe she has a man
in every port! I would. Why not? The nature of the work no doubt
allows it. Poor thing, though, not able to take care of a husband
because she's flying all over hell's creation. Freda twisted in her seat.
The woman's arms were big and had all kinds of nasty looking veins

in them. If worse comes to worse, this one can throw a few of us over a shoulder and jump down to earth. Freda closed her eyes, and the plane moved out across the runway. Dashing out some Our Fathers and looking wide-eyed at the lengthy one-storey buildings as they whipped past, Freda saw the angle change, then she was in the sky again. The plane's engines were roaring like a thousand old cars with their mufflers shot. She hoped the sound would die down when the plane straightened out, but it did not. The plane was a DC-10, an older one with its engines at the back, right behind Freda's seat. She did not care about the sound, not really. Being up in the air again was the main thing.

She needed to fart. The plane was crowded, but the seats in front and beside her were empty. She figured she might as well—they went and stuck her all the hell the way down here, alone. Anyway, with the racket of the engines, who would ever know?

Then, just when the smell of it was bringing her a smile and the seat belt sign was switched off, a fat man with several strands of coal-black hair was coming her way. He was pulling on the backs of the seats as he moved on his way to the toilet. Oh Jesus. When he got to Freda's seat, his nose twitched and eyes sharpened. He looked up at the sign that read, "toilet vacant." He lay the blame there. This'll be a circus, thought Freda.

The stewardess with the arms brought breakfast. Freda had eaten a bran muffin and boiled egg on the flight from Sydney to Halifax, but she kept quiet about this and, calmly, took the second breakfast as if it were her due. She was committing some heinous in-flight crime, she preferred to think, and if found out was certain they would bring the plane down in Montreal somewhere. They would toss her from the airplane and out on the runway; they wouldn't even bother to come to a full stop. From the Tarmac she would watch the big thing sail off to tear up the skies again. Abandoned on a Montreal airstrip with no dignity—and no suitcase—all because of this second breakfast!

Another bran muffin. But the eggs were scrambled, and they served more coffee, too. If I eat all this and get active, those little masks will come down.

She hoed into the food. The excitement of flying, the nearness to the bathroom, not knowing where she was going but not feeling bad about it either—it left her reckless. The eggs were tasty with salt. When she had finished, she blew on and sipped her coffee. The stewardess with the arms came and collected the tray.

"Hit the spot?" asked the stewardess.

"Bull's eye."

The passengers were told to fasten their seat belts for landing in Toronto, where, the captain said, it was "five degrees and sunny." That's summer for me, Freda said to herself. The plane made its descent, and she felt weightless. She watched as the wings were falling above the houses in Brampton, as she heard someone a few seats up say. Brampton, thought Freda. Don't I have a nephew living there, one who drives some kind of truck, with the wife who's a school teacher? I'll try to give them a call if I can, if they tell us to get off the plane. Everything depends on me for a change now. I do the calling and not the sitting around and waiting. This travelling business is not too bad at all.

The plane skipped in for a landing and the afterburners came on, sounding as if a big oil furnace had kicked in. Taxiing along the runways, Freda looked up at the seat belt sign. It was still on. Looking around and feeling devilish, she quietly reached down to undo her belt. If we are struck here on the ground, I'm sure I'll pull through. Leaving this seat-belt sign on after landing is just the captain's way of showing who is in charge, that's all. Then they hit a big bump, and she scrambled to clip the belt together. The plane bounced to the terminal, where it pulled up alongside another passenger chute. The captain's voice came out of the overhead speaker and thanked everyone for flying with Air Canada. He told those continuing west to Vancouver to stay on board as they were only on the ground long enough to pick up more passengers. Ah shit, thought Freda. She saw Wally make his way out, carrying his guitar. Good luck in the cooking racket, she silently wished him.

In front of her was a netted pouch holding magazines. One magazine showed pictures of gifts you could buy while flying. Mostly it was perfumes with silly names and clownish ties. She cleaned her eyeglasses in her sweater then had a good look around at the people coming on board. They were no different from the people back home. One face had a certain resemblance to Jack Peters, she thought. Another to his sister, Mary. And here comes Auld Philip Burke. Maybe that's what the world is made up of in the end, people from back home, and this plane is just a big flying bus setting down to pick them up all across Canada. How grand, she thought.

Then her seat partner appeared. She spotted him right away, and he spotted her right away. She could tell it was him by the pissed-off look he was sending down to her. He wore a trimmed beard, and his eyeglasses were thick, no rims, just little golden arms with clear-plastic nose bridge pieces. His hair looked like it was permed, but it didn't suit him. He was too old for it, and this was the hairstyle meant for someone friendly looking. If anything, it only soured his look further. He looks like no one I know, thought Freda.

He stood beside Freda's seat, looking hard at where he had to go, two seats in. He looked around for assistance, but no one came. Freda could tell what he was thinking: the seat was windowless, in a corner and beside an old woman; it would be unbearable for him. Little lines of worry were at the end of his nose. Take your seat, she thought, you big friggin baby. He moved, finally.

"I hope my bag is not in your way," said Freda, into his ass as it moved past her. She was apologizing for her suitcase, which was under her feet. She wanted to explain that all her things were in there, including her drawers, that she didn't trust it or them with anyone.

"Umm," was his only reply. A goddamned "umm," to an older woman, practically a senior! Freda looked up at him. How stupid am I, apologizing, being nice to him? she thought. One of those ties from the magazine would suit him…if he were dangling from it, she thought as the plane took off again. They were climbing out over central Canada, heading west. Freda thought about all the wheat that would soon be below and about all the flour that would be produced from it. Having baked bread all her life, she mentally saluted all the farmers here and was proud to be flying above them. She even turned and smiled at her seat companion, but he was in no shape to respond. His elbows were out, his hands flattened against his ears and pushing in on that nicely permed hair; he was being completely deafened by the roar of the engines. Perfect, thought Freda. That's just what he and his childish disposition need.

The plane levelled out and the seat belt sign went off. Someone was up again, coming toward the bathroom. Freda seized the opportunity to let another fart go, the second bran muffin having brought this one on. She keep it quiet, though, and remembered how her grandson Bradley classed these silent ones as SBDs. Silent-but-deadly. He's a wicked five-year-old, thought Freda, and will grow up to be a bad one.

Leaning forward to better spy on her seat companion, she pretended to be interested in the bright sky and the puffy clouds outside the window. The victory was decisive. She saw that Mr. "Umm" had his elbow protruding sharply and his right hand stopping up an offended ear; the other elbow was pressed against his ribs, his left hand pinching his nose. Freda saw him look up at the bathroom sign. Triumph, she thought, the same feeling she had after fixing the record player when no one else could (it had been only a matter of drawing back on the needle). Flying is beautiful, beautiful, and the world is fine. She looked at the other characters on board and had immediate love for them all, even this poor fellow beside her, pinching his nostrils. What an actor! Bravo! But his act won him attention then. The stewardess—arms almighty—was now in front of Freda's face, speaking across to the troubled man, the lines in his nose a tired sharp pink now.

"Sir? Sir? We're sorry about the noise," she said looking at him plug his nose. "There are no other seats available right now. We're going to ask the pilot if he can reduce the engine noise."

"Don't reduce it too much," said Freda, "unless you prove to us that there are springs on those beds of clouds down there."

"Pardon?"

Freda waved her hand. Obsequious tart, she thought. What about me? What about asking me if I need another seat or if the noise was too much? Just because this sulk is making a big show of things he gets catered to. Obsequious was one of Freda's favourites, but she could not remember if she got that one from *Reader's Digest* or off the soaps. It had been a hobby of hers to keep a dictionary near when the soaps were on. Tart—she didn't have to switch the TV on for that one. Ah, for the love of God, she thought, this same one who was going to fly me down to earth if anything happened, this woman who with a smart enough head on her shoulders to be working in the flying business was apologizing to this big child here beside me, and for what? It's not so bad. Why is he crying? The big sulk. Look at him now—he's pacified, reading a big novel that's a thousand pages or more. He's not even through a dozen pages. He probably just brought it aboard to show off to everyone that he's classy, make it look like he reads all the time. In all my born days never seen the likes. Mamma's boy. What's he going to ask for next, someone to hold his hand? Well, don't look this way, fella. I'm liable to break it if you put your hand this way. I don't make any fuss over engine noise. I let people do their jobs.

She stood up and went into the bathroom, and pushed the accordion door shut behind her. She got herself in position and thought, Definitely a toilet. Bathrooms are far bigger. Stripping off, she sat and thought about how vulnerable she was. If we crash now this'll be a fine way to find a woman, this'll be a nice finish to it all. Doing up her slacks again, she banged her elbow on the sink. Christ Almighty, there's not enough room to swing a mouse let alone a cat! Perhaps we can shrink that fellow out there and give him a good twirl, bang his head off the walls a few times. He probably has a tail.

She was thirsty but could find no cups. She bent over and got her mouth under the tap, taking good swallows because someone had told her that flying on a plane really dehydrated a person. Besides, she knew that water was the thing that kept a person young and spongy looking. The years make you haggard enough, she thought. Keeping a good supply of water in you is the only way to keep from looking all dried out like some old forgotten bread crust down behind a couch. And now, especially now, that I'm heading for the first time to the other side of Canada, I have to watch myself. I have to keep mindful on this trip.

CHAPTER 3

In the night Freda woke with something on her arm. She had sensed it even before she woke. A cockroach. Not a big one, but a cockroach. The building across the street was so brightly lit all night that Freda could see the insect poised on the end of the pillow, like a coal chip. When it scurried down to the mattress, she spied another on the white nightstand. Curling the fingers of her right hand into a fist, she bashed the second one with the fleshy part of her hand then scraped the remains on the edge of the table. She ripped the tightly tucked sheets open all the way down to her feet, then ran her hands over her body and scanned the bed. She again felt in through the armholes of her night dress. When she had put on a pair of socks she stepped onto the bathroom floor, which was elevated by about six inches. She felt along the wall for the light switch and turned it on. Her eyes squinted sharply but adjusted quickly. Scanning the dresser, closet, chair, TV stand, walls and curtains, the window, then again all along the bed, she could find nothing. Her eyes rested on her blue suitcase.

Stepping down off the bathroom floor, she moved along the night stand to her bed. She fully removed all the sheets and shook them. She also gave the heavy curtains at the window a good shaking. Nothing; just some hacking and spitting in a room down the hall, coming from the direction of the gnome's room—another of the hotel's creatures. The gnome was easily in his eighties but had the black eyes of a twenty-year-old, so he looked dangerous. He wore sweat pants, runners, and a crew-neck sweater. He haunted the halls, half-squatting as he walked, always toting a cigarette and knocking its ashes into a cupped hand. His bitterly taut face gave him the look of someone who spent a lifetime hating everything and everyone. At first, Freda had given him the benefit of her kind nature. He may have undergone some sort of nerve damage which scrunched up his face, she thought. You never know.

She had seen him after Bobby had let her off, as she was stepping out of the elevator and onto her floor. The bright light bulbs that hung from skinny electrical cords in the ceiling lit him harshly. A native woman was with him. Then Freda noticed an object sticking crossways in the gnome's mouth—something transparent, an instrument of some kind. With his free hand the gnome was slapping the inside of the woman's elbow. Something bad was happening and Freda wanted to pass them quickly. Up close she saw it was a syringe in his mouth. He slapped the woman's arm and continued looking hatefully at Freda.

Not until she had entered her room and locked her door did Freda realize that this is what they all talk about: these are the drugs they all take, she thought, and the gnome is mixed up in it! The whole scene became clear to her: he was the pusher! That woman begging in the street below, maybe that was what she was after the money for. Freda then remembered that outside, just below her room, was the rooftop of a vacant parking garage, covered with thick green moss. She looked out the window then. Little sticks all the same size, lying flat or sticking out as if planted by hand were all along the roof. They shone in the wet green of the moss. These are what they put in their arms, thought Freda, and then they toss them out the window. Perhaps they come here to kick the habit. Maybe this is a ritual dump site for those getting off it for good. Perhaps the hotel is filled with the best kind of heroes. But she knew that was ridiculous. There are no heroes here, just poor, pitiful people. The roof is only some grand display of their sloth. And cockroaches to top it off! Lord, give me strength.

She decided to take a bath. It was quarter past four in the morning, but there was no way she was going back to bed. When the tub was a quarter full, she stripped off and got in. She could feel the cold porcelain under her heels and buttocks. The big bear-paw tub was the best thing she had seen when she first saw the room; she thought that staying here would not be so bad as long as she had a tub to climb into and warm up in. She stretched herself out, trying to get under the water. The water was coming forcefully from the faucet, and the sound made her feel better.

Above the sink was a big medicine cabinet with a mirror angled down. Steam inched up the mirror, but she could still see the reflection of her room. The small black TV on its swivel stand was the only modern piece of furniture. Everything else was old, worthless. The plaster walls had cracked and warped. The bed was low and wide, with hard springs nearly poking through. The dresser had so many layers of paint on it that it was as thick as animal hide, and the armchair near it was low and strangely long—meant for someone who had either very long legs or perfect priestly posture. The curtains at the window were a dusty gold colour. They must have weighed fifty pounds apiece, but the weight was not without purpose: they helped turn away the cold, keep at bay the wet drafts that moved freely through the panes.

The water was now a good depth, and Freda reached over to turn off the faucets. Pulling herself up and reclining into the sloped back of the tub, she closed her eyes and listened to the drips from the closed faucet. Sounds of coughing and spitting grew louder and annoyed her. Freda pressed on the tub's sides and raised herself. She shook her arms to flick water from her upper body, and stepped out onto the thick bath towel she had used earlier. She walked out to get the remote control for the TV and to position the swivel stand where she might better see the reflection in the bathroom mirror. Switching on the TV next, she waited a moment for it to warm up. The room filled with grey light, and when the picture appeared two men were discussing the trial. One was fat and the skin in his neck quivered when he spoke, while the other wore thick glasses that sat on a nose sharp enough to open a tin of cat food.

Freda settled on the ethnic channel that broadcast information for new immigrants. Its screen was steady as a bulletin board, and there was classical music playing. I am a foreigner myself, she thought. Maybe the announcements and listings will give me some ideas about what to do here.

She got back in the tub and looked at the TV in the mirror. She could not read anything of course, but she listened to the classical music. A crescendo of hacking and spitting came from the halls now; the Granite Arch was waking. She slipped further down into the warmth of the bath but realized that the water was getting cold, so she hauled herself out again.

Drying herself with a hand towel, the only one still dry from the stack that had come with the room, she strode to the end of her bed and dressed in the same clothes she had worn the night before.

On her dresser was a bulb of garlic that she had brought across Canada; someone had told her a clove every morning prevented sickness. People kept their distance from that fellow, but he said it kept him healthy. The idea of getting sick so far away from home frightened Freda. If her breath was bad, fine; she knew only Wilena and Bobby out here anyway. To keep the odour at bay, her idea was to cut up every morning's dosage into tiny pieces with her grandson's Swiss Army knife. The little pieces would go down nicely with a glass of water, and there would be no need to chew. Yes, this knife is already coming in handy, she thought, taking it out of her purse. She thought of Bradley giving it to her. "Here, Grandma. In case you get lost, in case you have to knife someone out there," he had said. It was the same one Milton had given the boy the Christmas previous. She had taken it and walked into her bedroom to cry. She had realized then how desperately she did not want to go. But all Ingonish knew about the trip, and the ticket had been bought; she couldn't back down now.

And she didn't. Here she was, in the loneliness of a Vancouver morning, alone with the knife and putting it to use. Because it was true, she was lost. But she was also trying to find her way out. Peeling the garlic and cutting it on the surface of her palm, she thought that she would have a nice meal later to make herself feel better. When the pieces were small enough she raised her palm to her mouth, carefully scraping off all the garlic with her upper teeth. She drank the water and washed her hands to get rid of the juice.

She pulled open the heavy curtains, but the city was still idling in sleep. She saw flashing red lights at the intersection. It lit the place like an ambulance after an accident, but with no sound. Toward the mountains, she could see only a few lights in a distant fog. Then the draft coming in through the sides of the window got her attention.

"Dear Jesus," she said. The street below had not changed overnight: the filthy buildings still surrounded the lonesome intersection. The traffic light looked as if it was making the area breathe, slowly, rhythmically, like something that lives forever. The redness magnified the surroundings. It was all so large out there, so dark.

She remade the bed, and got under the covers with her clothes on. Hacking. Coughing. Spitting. Early risers, these drug addicts.

Reaching out from her bed and and turning the TV swivel, she switched on the TV and squinted at the grey light that again filled her room. An Asian family was sitting down to a table of food, and they were eating like pillaging Vikings. There was camaraderie among them; something important was being discussed. But their gorging carried on. Their clothes were the same as Americans; they even looked American, especially their hairstyles. And the bursts of speech, too; their clever responses—whatever they were! The scene was definitely North American. The TV screen switched and an announcement written in English appeared: Volunteers needed to teach English as a Second Language. In return volunteers would receive free Japanese, Korean or Chinese lessons. Freda thought she might be good at teaching English. She had the time; God knows she had always been fond of words. The advertisement said to contact the information desk at the Vancouver Public Library. A picture of the library came up on the screen—it was the same one she had asked the man in the elevator the directions to, the one she had walked past on the very first day but couldn't find again. She had stopped and looked up at it, and thought about all the books inside. Why the hell not volunteer? she thought.

She pulled the sheets around her neck. She had made up her mind to head to the library when the sun was up. She would inquire about signing up for this volunteer work if it killed her. Who knows how long I'll be here? And work, that's what a person needs, something to organize the time. Yes, work. Everything would be in order then; I could even meet people. Come on, sun, rise for the love of God, rise!

She sat up and swung her feet to the floor. On another channel, the morning newscasters were on, sitting with good posture and tidy faces. They were saying something about Bosnia. The three cleaning ladies must be up by now, she thought. They'll be leaving their apartments soon, catching their bus and making their way over here. Their day would be a series of rooms, changing sheets and getting towels. I need something like that. But God, the sights they must see here. I could not do what they do.

More of the trial came on. Freda and the accused were sharing the same time zone now. They were both awake and starting their day. Going to the window, she saw that the city was waking too and giving over to the day at last.

*

The light was finally getting in the room and scrubbing things up a bit, making it all look better. Freda put on her jacket and went to the door. Pulling it shut behind her and locking it slowly, she was careful again to put her key at the bottom of her purse. The smell in the hallway was better this morning, clinical, almost pleasant—it might have been the dampness. She caught sight of one of the cleaning ladies about to round the corner at the end of the hall, down by the toilet for the rooms with no bath.

"Good morning," Freda called.

The lady stopped and turned as if she had been caught doing something wrong. Towels were over her arm, and her expression was at first obedient but tough. She recognized who it was, and a generous smile loosened her look.

"Good morning for you. You awake up early!"

"Too cold to sleep," said Freda, trying to make a joke. The cleaning lady's face fell into a frown and both eyebrows peaked.

"You have cold?"

"I'm joking. I'm fine. I'm warm. Have a good day."

"I bring you blanket, yes? Thank you, bye." She continued on her way, disappearing around the corner. Freda used her knuckle to press the elevator button, and the big machine groaned on its way to fetch her. The doors opened and she went inside, but a young man's voice called out.

"Wait!"

She held the elevator, and he thanked her when he got on. He had a thin goldish beard but did not look dirty. There was no hair on top of his head, and that on the sides was as short as a cow's. He stood very mannerly and even advised against a chill that was supposed to be in the air this morning. His pants looked uncomfortably tight and were covered in a dried grey mud. He carried a big bag.

"Off to work?" said Freda.

"Yes. I do plastering. You were probably wondering what I'm carrying here. It's tools. The police stopped me one night about it." There was almost an elegance to his speech. The elevator doors opened and they stepped off.

"Have a good day at work," said Freda, and with the smile still on her face, she looked over at Reception. A different hotel clerk was on, one she had never seen; he didn't look at all intimidating. The young man said goodbye then bid the hotel clerk a good morning. His greeting was returned. The whole place was better suddenly. Freda said nothing, just kept to herself and followed the young man out into the street. But he was in a rush and she was quickly left behind.

People filled the streets. Everyone carried purses or bags, some both. They had their chins tucked in deeply to keep the cool air from their necks, and their foreheads seemed to lead them to where they were going. Freda looked up and could not see a hint of cloud. The sky had cleared and it was going to be a good day. But I must look strange standing here, she suddenly thought, looking up while the rest of humanity darts ahead not seeing anything around or above them. How wrapped up in things must people be, not to take notice of the morning sky!

Extra-long buses and heavy trucks were out now. Men in hard hats, standing around muddy, walled-in job sites, were drinking coffee and talking, their dirty gloves making their cups look delicate. Some had their hair hanging down behind their hats. Oh, how I hate that, Freda said to herself. It makes them so dirty looking. If they only knew. Just for a day I wish I had the authority of a dictator so I could send people with clippers out into the streets, ten haircutters on each street would do. Shave all the heads of these beatniks, I'd say! Give the whole city a brush cut!

She walked along Pender Street to Thurlow, where she turned right and headed for the water. Everything was brightening up, and when she was crossing the last big street before Canada Place, the sun came over the Coast Mountains and lit a big rectangle in the street. When she reached the observation decks, breathing in the morning air, Freda felt stronger. This is what I came across the country for, this air, the mountains. She looked up and saw that the jagged mountain tops appeared to rip apart the skyline, and tear east. Snow was on them, and behind, the blue backdrop was marvellous.

Below trains were snaking into a station to deposit tired passengers. All the busy lives, thought Freda. How much must get done with all these people. She listened and could hear the whinge and whine of the trains, slowing and speeding. The sun hit patches of snow alongside the tracks and was reflected in the frosty train windows, which seemed to wink up at Freda.

"Morning!" she called down.

The helicopters came in from the mountains and chopped across the bay to their landing platforms near the tracks. They hovered, then set down slowly like bees on a large flower. They let a few men off before lifting and settling back into the air again, rising up into the mountains to fetch more people. They must be carrying the rich, thought Freda, rich businessmen probably. How fast life must go when you have all that money. It must just go up and down, like a ball thrown in the air.

Seaplanes, too, came down like heavy insects to light in the ripples of the bay. They had to yank their big rears fully out of the water before climbing back into the air. Their big buzzing was all over the place, and sounded like dragonflies in a jar. More businessmen, thought Freda. Busy and rich, the best clothes, the most vicious faces, the softest hands, the most dangerous fingers. Ah, enough of this foolishness, she told herself. You know better than to go on like this. They could be the nicest of people aboard these planes, people nice enough to meet and get to know.

Walking around to the north decks of Canada Place, she heard more clearly the car horns sounding off at a distance. She could see ferries on this side, their windows shut for the trip across the bay. She thought of the Englishtown Ferry during the ride from Ingonish to Sydney. Freda liked to get out of the car on the ferry, winter or summer. It always broke up the journey so nicely. She liked to breathe the air there, too, and look over the side. A drop or two of seawater was sure to splash up at her, and she liked it.

Other people were on the observation decks. Freda could smell their cigarettes, which were different from what folks smoked back home. There was an Asian man and his pretty Asian girlfriend with him; they were wearing expensive looking coats with strips of animal fur that came down buttoned-up fronts. The jackets were open at the neck, though, and their throats looked awfully cold. Neither had much flesh on the bones, which didn't help to improve matters. They had a little green disposable camera with them and were snapping pictures of each other. They saw Freda and began looking over shyly.

"Give it here," she said.

They didn't understand. She put out her hand. They passed it over, then bowing said: "Sank you wery much." They stood at attention and smiled beautifully. Freda made sure she got the mountains in, and the camera snapped the shot. Coming forward, they thanked her again.

"Where are yas from?" asked Freda, but they seemed dumbfounded. "I said, where are you from? Your country?"

"Country?" they repeated. "Country...Ah, Japan! We are Japan!" They both smiled and looked very happy to have said something in English.

"Hello, Japan," said Freda. "That's great. Well, enjoy yourselves here in Canada."

The couple waved to her, even though they were standing very close to Freda. Then, bowing as they moved, went away happily. Why can't the rest of mankind be like that, thought Freda. Grateful, full of life. And so well groomed. She thought of her plan to volunteer and was looking forward to it now. She felt akin to foreigners suddenly, because she was not from here either. She felt protective of them.

Making her way down the shadowed side of the overhead decks, she stepped aside for people ascending the stairs and ramps on their way to the big decks. Yas're a little late, she thought. The sun's up and the show's over! She could see a marina with lots of boats out in front and a big green park in the backgroud. She could make out people walking, some looked to be jogging. I will go and get something to eat in the park, she thought. The weather is nice; I can go to the library after.

It was cool in the shadows of Canada Place. A cruise ship was docked abreast the wide walkway; workers were driving forklifts in and out of a large opening in the bottom of the ship, carrying boxes of oranges. The loads just kept coming. Freda figured it must all be for juice because there was no way they could eat all those oranges. But then of course there's scurvy, she thought, and ships must feel the need to be prepared. She would get some of her own oranges later. Walking the length of the ship then looking back and tracing her eyes along its long broad side, she paused. It's a mall! she thought. They'll never believe this back home!

Three Asians were in a tiny rubber boat slung over the ship's bow, standing and holding big squeegees. Window washers, dangling a good fifty feet above the harbour. Expensive looking life-jackets were over their shoulders and because of the smallness of the space their faces were almost pressed up against each other's. The three wore very nice moustaches that were the same colour as their eyes; their hair was a lovely healthy black, and short.

"Catch anything?" she called over. They looked in Freda's direction, then laughed. Freda smiled back, and waved before moving on.

The temperature was climbing and walking felt good. But the park was much farther than it had looked from the decks. When Freda reached the entrance she was tired and needed a place to sit. Everyone was wearing fancy sports clothes and dark sunglasses. She sat on a bench to rest for a few moments then started off again, but she knew her stroll had become a journey. It was so beautiful here, though, so flat, clean. She sat at another bench. The salt air was heavy on her lips and she felt it on the backs of her hands; mixed with the smell of the cedar trees nearby, it was especially pleasing.

The trail wound along the water to a rise where a big bridge disappeared from view in the trees. The bench she was sitting on had a metal plaque with an inscription:

"This bench is dedicated to the walkers of Stanley Park in memory of Glady and Mavis Blanchard. Please enjoy the walk and view."

I am, Glady and Mavis, I sure am, Freda thought. She noticed that other benches had inscriptions, too. Any outdoor furniture Freda had ever known in Ingonish bore inscriptions of Parks Canada, but it was strange to find out that a community existed here in the big city of Vancouver. Another sign said, "Seawall." Two older Asian men near the sign were squatting down and resting on the backs of their ankles. Their posture looked queer and a little lewd. They were silently smoking and pulling on lines they had in the harbour. They were fishing, with bare hands and fishing twine. Surely to God they wouldn't eat what they caught here, thought Freda.

"Catch anything?" she called over. They looked in her direction, then bobbed their heads and squinted their eyes. Freda smiled back, and waved. They returned to their cigarettes and lines.

A container ship was travelling fast through the harbour, which did not look big enough to accommodate it. Freda remembered when the *Queen Elizabeth 2* had stopped at North Bay. Lots of young girls from Inverness, Cape Breton, were on board with bagpipes and wearing Scottish piping uniforms. They were lovely to look at and people from all over—North Bay, South Bay, and even from down north—were there. Milton had taken Freda over that day. He was excited because he had been aboard the boats in the war. He had caught sight of the ship first thing that morning as it rounded the bill of Smokey, before it was even light.

Driving home after seeing it in North Bay, he was still excited. He had said, 'There were more cars lined up over there than when the ice cream truck went off the road down at the Keltic! I'm going to take us away on one like that someday, Freda. You watch.' He winked, flipped his sun visor down, then back up. The sun visor had always been part of the car's operation for him; even in the winter he frigged with it, Freda recalled. How excited he would be now if he were here, with the size and speed of everything, the plane ride out.

She started off again. It was cloudy now and the trail seemed deserted. The occasional rollerblader whizzed past. If she was lucky, she heard them coming and gave over the whole path to them. She was not always fast enough, though, and they would tear past, scaring her. Selfish bastards, she thought. I hope yas trip.

At last she came to a twist in the trail where it passed under the bridge she had seen earlier. She heard a queer noise here. A green brass plaque read Lion's Gate Bridge. Big knots and cuts were in the cables and in the steel of the bridge's underbelly. The queer noise was the sound of incessant traffic sailing over the bridge; it was particularly mournful.

From here to the next stone distance marker, she did not stop, which made it six miles of park she had covered. Her feet were undeniably sore. Still, the air and the scenes remained lovely, and her biggest joy was to know that she had found a good place to come again. The open water of the ocean came into view next, and the plaque here read "English Bay." There were more people suddenly, but the languages sounded anything but English. A good dozen or more container ships, like the one she had seen earlier, were in the bay. They sat heavy and silent, the same way the buildings of the city sat.

She looked for some clue that would tell her where she was in the park now—if this was still, in fact, the park—but she found nothing. Any bearings she had were gone; the landmarks were long gone; also, her feet were gone. Just then, the sight of the city buildings restored her to a better feeling. She looked and saw there was still plenty of sun and she had her purse with her. There is nothing to worry about, she told herself.

The Seawall curved along two beaches and a large children's play area. People everywhere talked in unnaturally loud voices, in unrecognizable languages. It seemed they had come here to talk, to get out of their homes, get some exercise, enjoy the sun. None of this was bad to see.

Then the city came down to the sand and here also were huge logs splayed out as if an audience for the tides. They were scattered over the beach, nearly covering it. People were propped up against the oceanside of the logs, some sleepily gazing out at the water, others with books in their laps. This is pretty good for February, thought Freda.

Near one log, she could smell the strong rotten scent of burning marijuana. Then, because of how the trail twisted, she was able to see who was smoking it: a man, rail thin, with hair that was tied back like in the old pictures of Chinese peasants. He wore pants only, rolled up at the cuffs.

It isn't that warm, thought Freda. Beside the man, two children with their hair tangled like clumps of seaweed were playing around a clothesline that was strung from the log to a clump of alders. Hippies, Freda figured. Living on a beach, in winter! That'll be the end of it, she thought. A woman, then a second, stood up from behind another log. Their hair was short, but they were very lovely. Ah, leave all this alone, Freda told herself. Take care of yourself. They're no different from any of the rest of us. There's no harm in them, and they are probably the friendliest people anyone would ever want to meet. She could now see where the path ended.

The trail met a street, and she was finally able to take her leave of the Seawall and step up into the city again. She came across a water fountain with a silver spout that stuck up. The thing looked just like a silver penis. Is it just me, or does it look like this to others? What pervert designed this? Is there no sense anymore? No respect for a woman? Although mortified, Freda was too thirsty to be proud. She was damned thirsty, she realized, and after glancing right and left, she took a good long drink.

Ever so slowly, she started to walk up Denman Street. All kinds of shops lined this street, and many vendors were selling their wares on the sidewalk. They did not leave much space to walk. Sidewalk coffee shops were filled with young men looking up from their drinks, men who looked to be in the prime of their lives; they were sitting leisurely, enjoying themselves, looking like well-fed young lions. Freda was amazed. Is there no work? Are yas all rich out here, is that it? They wore their hair short, though, this bunch. They were presentable, with clean faces and good posture.

Freda kept her eye on them and noticed how they smiled with big pouty lips at everyone going by in the streets. She smiled back at one or two but did not feel overly friendly towards them. Why the hell aren't yas out trying to earn a dollar? It's the middle of the day, for Christ's sake! Was everyone suddenly on vacation or travelling as she was? Oh, I'm tired, she said to herself. My mind is starting to go.

She came to a pizza shop. Her feet were really tender now and she knew she had gone too far. Two Dollars a Slice, read one sign at the doorway. Here we go, she said to herself, that's the real price anyone should have to pay for a meal. She went inside and stopped at a small glass case just inside the entrance. Large pizza slices were on display, and they rotated with about as much speed as she had climbed the street with. The food was made sunny looking by a heat lamp. She had to step aside as a couple was leaving arm in arm and would not let go of each other. Saying sorry, she realized that it was two men. So, this is the game, she thought, then looked back out toward the coffee drinkers on the sidewalk.

She ordered a slice with the works. It came to almost two-fifty with tax, which was still a bargain. She sat near the window and ate slowly. When there was only the crust remaining, she knew she was full but she wanted to eat more to keep up her strength.

The girl who served the pizza had a British accent and was as skinny as an electric cord, but not unhealthy looking. Her classy speech compensated for any meekness she might have had. Freda could not recall ever having heard a British accent in Cape Breton, which was peculiar, as the islands were so much closer geographically. Why would they skip over the Maritimes and come all this long way out to Vancouver?

Freda turned toward an open window. It had grown chilly. This had been too much for one day. She would have to watch herself, her defences could easily get worn down. After saying a little prayer in apology, she ate the rest of her pizza.

She was glad she had gone on the walk; she had found Stanley Park and had been around the Seawall. Where she was now she had no idea, but the long walk had given her a great sense of accomplishment. The Seawall would be her retreat, a nice flat place along the sea, with lots of people around. Best of all, she had found it on her own. This was why she had not gone to Wilena's directly; she liked her independence. Yes, the Seawall was hers—a good place, one to count on.

Her meal was over. She held the paper plate and found herself contemplating the men sitting in the coffee shops along the street. They were in little groups and smiling out to passersby while maintaining their good postures. Oh, their hair looks so much better than that long dirty stuff. But they all look like children, as though they have been dressed by over-caring mothers, she thought. And the styles of clothing—collars big, floppy shirts with little zippers at the throat. None of that—the ritual—can be easy, thought Freda. Freda turned from the street scene.

"Great slice of pizza," she said to the British girl, who had just then bobbed her head up from below, like a partridge. But her face looked to be on the verge of tears.

"What's wrong?" said Freda, holding out the paper plate for her to take away.

"Nothing, nothing. That's just the way my face is. I've always been a little over-tender in my gaze. My mother said that she didn't bear me, but rather that I stepped out of a painting at the museum one day and she took me home with her." Her face brightened.

"I agree. You have lovely looks. Are you from England?"

"I am, yes. A little place in the south called Devon."

"What are you doing all the way over here?"

"Work, travel. It's not so easy to get a job in England right now. Bloody reign of you-know-who." Her expression hardened.

"But why did you come all the way out here and not stop somewhere more east, like Nova Scotia? That's a good place for you, closer to home. You shot right past all the fun."

Then, as though she'd met a friend from childhood, the girl's face beamed. "That must be where you're from then, is it? Well, perhaps I will make a trip out there one day."

A customer was perusing the big menu that hung above the girl. Freda watched the girl's expression. What a lovely girl, she thought.

"So long," Freda said, getting up.

"Wait...Okay. Good bye, but do come again. This is my own shop, and I'm just getting it up and running." The new customer was taking his time with the menu, so the girl came over and said to Freda, "We'll talk when you come again. I'm getting tired of all these oddballs coming in here and never saying noffin." She looked at Freda, tilted her head in the direction of the customer, and winked fully.

"I'll talk to you," he said to her. "Come on. I'll listen to whatever you say and better yet, I'll agree with it."

Freda winked. He turned out to be a good one and provoked a big grin from the British girl, who burst out in the true ringing laughter of someone who had kept to herself too long. Her back teeth showed; her whole frame shook. Then there was a silence, but the laughter returned and infected everyone in the shop. Freda, feeling responsible, left before it subsided. Always leave them laughing, she told herself as she walked out the door.

CHAPTER 4

Out in the street Freda leaned over a chain railing. She had trouble getting attention, so she interrupted a conversation.

"I know you fellas don't work, but maybe one of yas can give me some directions. Where's the new library?"

"The big one on Robson? With the Roman columns?

"Yes."

"They haven't finished it yet."

"I just want to find it. There's an information desk there I need to get to."

"Well, I don't know about that."

One fellow stood and came over to Freda. "You take this road to Robson and hang yourself a right when you come to..."

"Pender!" another said. Freda paid attention to the man standing.

"Yes, Robson to Pender, I guess. Yes, it's there. You'll see it anyhow, it's tall and brand new." He sat with his friends again but, still looking up, said, "It's a bit far. I'd grab a bus."

"I'll make it. Robinson to Pender you say."

"*Robson.*"

Freda left them to their coffee and talk and went back the way she had come. People filled the sidewalks; cars filled the streets. Freda found herself stepping out of the way and sometimes even stopping to let faster-moving people pass, but when she did, no one would let her back into the flow. She soon wisened up. Let a collision come, she told herself, I don't care. Suddenly someone smashed into her from behind. Ah, to hell with it all, she thought and barged ahead like a bull, abandoning any strategies.

This part of town was tidier than where she was staying. Shops were newer, buildings lower, and the younger people looked better fed. There were still bums and tramps, however. And everyone here walked past them with glazed eyes. She was doing the same, but kept at least one eye on them. She soon realized that she'd better stop this, because they were very clever. They came up to her when they saw her looking—some would even cross over to her from the other side of the street. One approached with spit and cuts on his mouth, and it sickened her. They saw that she was not blind to them but sympathetic, that she was from away. In her first two days, she had given money out but stopped when she took account of how much it was costing her. She tried to change her manner to that of one of the cool creatures, one of these other passersby who had become oblivious to the panhandling. She attempted to become citified. Can I have some change?...Could you help a guy out with some coffee?...I need fare for the bus to get home. It didn't take her long to tire of it. But those damn pitiful looks. Those sorrowful eyes, and the wrinkled, scarred skin. They will break me, she thought. If they push only a little more, they will break me.

On Robson Street, near the fancy clothing shops and bigger build- ings, she saw a man sitting right out on the sidewalk. Staring past the many legs, pant cuffs, and shoes treading by, he was sitting the way a woman at a picnic might, legs tight together and off to one side, one arm fully extended to prop up his body. Covering his legs and up to the waist was a child's sleeping bag, thin, brown, identi- cal to the one that Freda had bought for her son Billy the time the Scouts were sleeping out at Broad Cove campgrounds. He needed it. But when he got home the sleeping bag was covered in sticky, mashed-up marshmallow, and spruce needles were all through it. Freda screeched at him; she said she would have to throw it out. She had been too rough with him, but the marshmallow was like glue; even after washing it twice in hot water, it was no better. It kicked around the house for years, then ended up out in the wood-shed and there it remained till it was ragged and torn, long after Billy was gone. But here was one just like it, looking brand new, and giving a homeless man some comfort on a sidewalk.

This man did not have his hand out like the others. He did not speak. A cardboard sign leaning up against a big tin coffee can was all he had. On the cardboard was written: Please Feed The Home-Less. He had a dog with him, a German shepherd that shared half his sleeping bag. Both man and dog twisted their heads to look in the same direction, as if they were staring out to sea, and as if they were the only two in the whole world.

Freda crossed the street at the next intersection and walked back to where she could see them better. Yes, this fellow was different; he had no direct approach, but quietly and simply existed as he was. There was something admirable in his letting fate take care of it all. And how dignified he looked. His hair was long but not offensively, a rainy-day silver colour, combed ever so neatly and with a care-fully drawn part. Even here, from the other side of the street, Freda could see the blueness of his eyes, the colour of the ice on Ingonish harbour after a good old-fashioned spring rainstorm, the kind that hits just before the ice leaves for good.

She started back across the intersection, back past the idling cars and shoppers, back to the man and his dog. She marched right up and put two loonies into the man's tin—one was for the German shepherd. The man took a moment to look up.

"Thank you."

"Are you warm enough?"

"My name is John," he said. "This is Isaac." He had his hand on the animal's back. Freda looked at Isaac. What is this business of naming animals after people out here?

"How did you come to it?" she said.

The dog sat up. It was a beautiful creature.

"Headed out west." He was a slow talker and looked off when he spoke.

"Is it hard? It must get cold."

"You're the first to ask that. Oh, I know about cold."

There was another drop into his can. Freda bade him farewell and continued up Robson.

She needed to get off her feet again and decided to stop in at a coffee shop—which was no problem as they were everywhere. One place even had a second outlet right across the intersection. She went in and ordered a small coffee. One dollar and sixty cents—Jesus, Mary and Joseph, she thought, I'll be out there with Isaac and John in no time.

Taking her coffee, she went over by a window and got into a chair that someone had just left. The chair was warm and felt as if it had been in use a long time. Clasping the sides of her cup with both hands, she drank, blowing and sipping, taking in a little at a time.

The sidewalks on both sides were jammed with people; the streets were just as tight with cars and buses creeping past. Where are they all going? Surely this is not all shopping. And how many Orientals are there, or is it Asians?...Orientals, Freda decided; it had a better ring to it. But what a slew! They have to make up fifty percent of the crowd. She watched them go by and knew they were not tourists by the strained looks on their faces. I bet life is even more crowded where they come from, she thought. This place is probably a break for them. But is it the land or the school they're here for? And with the unemployment rate up where it was, with the homeless—how did things work out for them? And the cost of everything? The dollar must be high where they're from. That's what it is. She swallowed more of the expensive coffee and when she was finished with the cup took it to the counter. The workers looked bewildered.

"A person can't bring the cup back?" she asked.

"We have people hired to do that."

Freda looked but said nothing. She walked out of the shop. The little bastards, she thought, trying to browbeat me. Is there no proper treatment of anyone anymore, even someone trying to do a good turn?

It was late afternoon when she made her final push up Robson Street to the library. Feeling winded, she worried that she might never walk again. Then, there they were, the Roman columns! The library! The sun was everywhere suddenly and warm on her back.

The library was tall like a tower, and looking up at its height made Freda feel as if she were on the roof looking down. Some men, installing a very large pane of glass, were guiding it to a big square opening as it was being lowered from a crane. The glass looked large enough to cover an ice rink. Freda supposed the men had Indian blood in them to be working up so high. She had read where Indians had no fear of heights, and it had been such a peculiar detail that it had always stayed with her. The article had stated that they were hired to clean the windows of the world's tallest buildings.

Shuddering, she looked down at the stone tiles of a promenade to get her balance. The tiles were a pretty colour and design, pink like baby skin, each one cut in the shape of an arrowhead. Now, this is the type of work I could do. I could easily sit out here all day and work installing tiles, arranging each one to fit nicely. She saw herself then sitting with a trowel in one hand and tile in the other, working on the surface of the promenade as if it were a giant puzzle. She had always enjoyed puzzles. The library itself, she thought, especially the top, I will leave to the Indians. But the ground I can do myself, clean and flat. Jesus himself would be able to stroll over it in his bare feet when I'm done. "Good work," he'd say, treading lightly, his robe gently trailing across the tile. "You could eat off of it, Jesus," Freda would say. Oh God, I'm losing my mind, she thought. I need a seat.

The main doors of the library were locked, but there was a glass door off to the side. Some office workers were inside. Freda went in and discovered that the room was very large.

"The library won't be open till October. We're Administration," a tall, masculine woman said.

"I saw on TV that yas were looking for ESL teachers, I think they're called. Teachers for the foreigners. To teach them to talk."

"Oh, I see. Newly-arrived Canadians, yes. Behind you, the bulletin board there. Have a look at it on your own. The large blue notices on top..."

"Look," Freda said, "I'm only here to help and I don't care for that tone your using with me, not one bit."

"We're busy getting the library set up here. I'm sorry if..."

"Yeah, well, that's still no way to treat a person."

Freda turned to look at the board and felt the gaze of everyone in the room on her. That was better, she thought. Another browbeater, but this one didn't get so far. No sir.

"Excuse me. You'll be interested in these, too." The tall woman was back, passing Freda a sheet of paper with information on it.

"Thanks," said Freda. Now, go on back to the little hole you crawled out of if you're finished sucking up. Jesus, the likes of that! If she wants to go toe to toe, I'm ready. I'm just in the mood to strangle someone.

As Freda turned to look at the bulletin board, someone else, shorter, came in from outside and started reading the notices.

"You want learn Chinese?"

"Pardon?"

"Chinese. You want to learn or not?" It was a girl who looked to be about fourteen, Oriental, wearing a big pair of glasses. She was talking to Freda just as bold as brass. Freda looked toward the staff. Paper shuffled.

"I can learn you..."

"I heard you. No, English is enough for me, let alone Chinese."

"Please, once again."

"Once again what? Oh, I need to sit."

"I am student. I teach you Chinese; you teach for me English."

The girl pointed to the notice board where Freda had been looking. Several of the notices were for language exchange: Korean for English, Japanese for English, Chinese for English, Hungarian, Arabic....The notices were mostly homemade with thin strips of telephone numbers on them.

"I can teach to you. Can, can!"

"I believe you! I believe you! Let's go back outside, so a person can sit." They went out the door, but the girl's heavy bag got caught up in the handle. Getting her untangled created a racket, but Freda saw that no one looked up from their desks.

"You looks very tired," said the girl outside.

"I am," said Freda. "I just only walked half the way around this city today. What did you say your name was?"

"My name is Pei-Jung."

"Pay Rug?"

"Pei-Juuung! You can just say me, Pei. Like, 'Pay Money.' You know?"

"Pay Money. I like it, but your English is not so bad already. What could I do?"

"No! It very bad! It have a lot of difficult with English."

"Well, first off, I am not a teacher, but I'll help out if I can. And I am only here in Vancouver for a little while. If I help, it's mostly just to stay busy. Understand? Not teacher, ok?"

"Ha, ha. Okay. We can talk only. Is good for me. You know?"

Freda liked her. She was as direct as a hornet. So honest and sincere, she seemed. Her hair was cut like a boy's, bangs straight across. It was a shame. And the glasses she had on—things mad scientists would wear, black rimmed and hard like burnt fudge.

"Okay, Pay Money. We'll..."

"No! Not Pay Money! Just Pei, only."

"Take it easy, don't have a tizzy on me! Jesus."

"What's your name?"

"I'm Freda."

"You seems like very kind woman, Freda."

"I'm all right. I try my best."

"When can you teach?"

"When? Anytime."

"Tomorrow okay?"

"All right then."

"You can come my house. It is near to here. You know?"

"No, I don't know. Know what? You keep asking me that, know....Your house, is that what you mean? How can I know where it is, when we just met?"

It took a moment for Pei-Jung to understand Freda's reply, but once she did, she laughed very hard. Freda glimpsed large flat teeth like a horse's. Pei was embarrassed and raised her hand immediately to cover her mouth.

"You come here and we meet here together. After, we go my house," she said.

"Fine enough. When, the afternoon?"

"No, afternoon, cannot! I am very busy in afternoon! Morning only, okay?"

"Yes, your Highness."

They agreed on ten, at the same spot. Pei-Jung said good bye, and walked off. Not looking back, she hoisted her big bag to her shoulder as any soldier fresh for a war would do.

*

Freda lingered outside the library a moment longer and watched as the wind created eddies of dust on the promenade, especially where it met the sides of the building. Small wrappers blew about. Evening was not far off; the sun had ducked behind some buildings. The sky was a cooler, wetter blue now that the clouds had rolled in. Freda decided to get something to eat before returning. There was not so much as a crust of bread back in her room, and when she finally made it back there she knew she would be in for the night. She got up and started along a street.

Feeling good about meeting Pei-Jung, this last leg of her day went nicely. What a little package of dynamite that young girl is! she thought. It should be fun getting to know her. It's my first time ever to speak to a Chinese person.

The streets were nearly empty of pedestrians and the area suddenly looked rough. The smell of piss was everywhere. It smelled the same way out in front of her hotel, too. Cutting a corner, she saw a hand-painted sign which looked to be the work of a three-year-old: Jerusalem Desserts, it spelled out. Bean Soup, two bucks a bowl. Bean soup it will be, she thought, and headed inside.

Gazing into a large run-down room, she hesitated at the entrance. Do I have my knife on me? she thought. She looked around till her eyes had adjusted to the light better. When they did, she realized the room was chock-full of hippies, and there was more hair than Rapunzel ever had. It hung from faces and from scalps and was as common as hayfields, except that neither rake nor pitch fork could ever get through these tangled masses. She saw the cook, near the pots, wearing an apron. He was the worst. A great lion's mane covered his head. But the girl beside him had her hair all lopped off. What's wrong with the world, thought Freda. The poor girl looked as though she had just undergone preparation for surgery, but she was standing there as natural as anything. A young girl, living under a stark head like that! Even worse, she had three nose rings looped through a nostril. And they were all staring at *her*, as if she were the odd man out.

"Soup! Bean soup," Freda called out from the door. The lion mane cocked his head to smile, then acted on the request. He went to a big pot, lifted up a caked ladle, and stirred what appeared to be a very thick mixture inside. He looked back at Freda and winked. But he does have lovely skin, thought Freda. I have to admit that. And his smile is very charming. So when this place does break apart with someone firing a chair against the wall and shouting, Fight! or when they do pull me to the floor, roll up my sleeve and cry: Hey! Let's get some dope in the old one, I'll look to him for assistance.

"Help yourself!" he called over, nodding his head down at the soup. He had been merely stirring it for her. *Help yourself*, that was the idea. Fine enough. There were assorted bowls beside the big pot. This must be an aspect of that communal spirit these people always operate in. And why the hell not. Taking up the ladle and moving her purse strap further up her arm, she began to dish up a bowlful. But by God, it smells good, she said to herself as she watched the soup go in. And it looks safe enough. She knew they had their eyes on her again and were looking more intensely than ever, but, strange though it was, she did not give one damn about any of them anymore. She was hopeful that the soup would turn out to be good. If she was right, she could come here again and again to get her meals. And that would be another problem gone.

She carefully set the ladle back down against the pot's side. When she looked up, she caught sight of the walls. They were covered in paintings with scenes from the Bible. "Jerusalem" was written below the biggest scene, in which three men in turbans were seated on the ground, apparently in conversation. Clay buildings were in the background. The painting was beautiful. Freda took a seat under it, where no one else was sitting. The painting brought her the same feeling of security as sitting under the stations of the cross back home. God himself will come out of the artwork and defend me if there is any trouble from this point. Let them try to stick me with their needles then. She remembered the fellow with the Bible in the hotel and looked around to see if he was here.

Taking off her jacket, she pulled her chair toward the food but then realized she had no spoon. She went to the counter but the lion mane was busy with a customer and the transaction was taking too long. Her soup was getting cold. She turned to one of the customers, who, well into his soup, looked to be enjoying his very first meal after having returned from a lengthy trip to the wilds.

"Where do I get the spoons?" she asked him.

The man had heard but did not answer. With prolonged drama, he set his own spoon against the inside of his bowl, then raised a napkin to his lips. He tapped his mouth. Come on, for the love of God! Freda eyed his red hair and big sloppy beard. Talk, you big galoot, talk! There must be a mouth in there somewhere! She had turned to look for someone else when he made a long crane-swoop movement with an extended hand. His fingers pointed to a grey plastic tray next to the soup pots. In plain sight! Ah, for frig sakes! I could have found them myself! Freda thanked him, but he only looked forward and held still.

Grabbing the cleanest spoon she could find, and one an appropriate size (some were big as ladles and others small as teaspoons), she returned to her chair, gave the spoon a clandestine wipe with a paper napkin, and plunged into her meal. The soup had lost some of its heat, but not its flavour. By Jesus it's good, she thought, then took spoonfuls of it slowly, because she was also trying to rest a little.

Other customers came in and, without batting an eye, scooped out their soup in one glop; then they took their seats calmly. That's how I'll do it when I come here from now on, thought Freda, realizing that she was feeling at ease, enough to scrutinize all exits and arrivals as she ate.

She contemplated the man who had indicated the location of the spoons. He had killed someone. She was sure of it. With his elbow on the table now and leaning his head into the crook of his thumb and two fingers, he looked to be very troubled. He was either in deep thought, or else the soup was tearing up his insides. What have I done to him? she thought. Have I caused this, asking for the spoon as I did? It must have triggered something, and he is going to go berserk at any moment. I reminded him of his long-dead mother, perhaps, the one he beat to death with a spoon. It must be that. Yes, as a boy, when he was calling out one night for something to eat his supper with, the antidepressants his mother was on were affecting her hearing so his pleas from the kitchen went unanswered. Fed up, he went to the first drawer in the kitchen and beat her senseless with the first thing he found, stopping only when her leg jerked for the last time. He fed himself then, finishing in the same unsettling pose he has now. Which was how the police found him—at the supper table, head in hand, and not saying a word.

Freda ate the last bit of her supper hurriedly, paid, and left.

The buses were driving with their lights on in the dusk. Freda was truly exhausted now and took no notice of the three men she was walking close behind. They were going in her direction. They were going too slowly but not slow enough so that she could pass. Glancing up at the revolving restaurant atop the Harbour Front Hotel, she tried slowing even more to let the men get ahead.

Relax, she told herself. It's nothing; they aren't looking back at you anymore. Then her hotel came into view, and she knew she would be fine. Cutting through a very small park tucked in behind the hotel meant she would save a lot of time and trouble. Freda had come through this way a few times and never minded, despite the scatter of bums that always slept in it. She was so tired, and needed to go to a bathroom right away. So she entered the park, still behind the men.

Oh, my legs are bad, she thought. But still, a good day—Stanley Park, the Seawall, the library, that little Chinese girl. Pay, Pay....She had her eye on the hotel when the three men in front broke apart. Two headed for a nearby bench and immediately began ripping open a garbage bag they had been carrying. The other slowed so that Freda was directly behind him. Slick as a dancer, he wheeled around and dipped his hand into the pocket of his jacket, taking out a knife. The blade was slim, and hardly visible in the night. He looked down at it, then up at Freda. He began to pick his fingernails, and stared hard at her like a sick, nasty cat. He might have been smiling.

But her legs—they wouldn't go! It was in her knees, they had shut down. The sight of the open knife had power over her, and she could not move.

She bowed. What else could she do? It was not a reaction she knew, but it felt natural enough now. More important, it was a gesture that told him that she realized her mistake, that she knew where she was and all about the rules that existed here. It was the honest mistake of an old lady and she was heartily sorry for it.

The greasy fellow bowed back. Freda slowly moved ahead, ignoring this revolt of her knees as they carried her poorly in a wide berth around the man. He was letting her go, but there was something not right in her chest now—as if the blade of the knife that she too well imagined were lodged there. Why the Christ is it taking so long to get out of this park? And why did you do that to me, knees? Are you that old and worthless? She heard her feet hit the sidewalk again.

In the hotel she did not even look toward the front desk, though she knew they were goddamn well watching her. She stepped inside the elevator that was waiting for her, and the machine climbed. She stared up at the buttons. When number three lit up, it stopped. But Freda was slow to get out, and she got jammed between the closing doors. Frightened, she ran for her room, for her life. She saw herself an old woman in an empty hallway, running through it—not neat, not swift, not clever, just old. Her key was in the lock, then she was inside. She sat on her bed and the hateful room that surrounded her seemed to laugh out loud. She switched on the TV, found the news. She found her rosary in the pocket of her winter jacket, then knelt beside the bed. Her day was done and she was crying.

CHapteR 5

At nine the next morning, Freda was sitting at a coffee shop called Corkie's drinking coffee to help rinse away the taste of garlic. She was eating a power muffin, a speciality of the shop. It contained raisins, dates, bran, and oatmeal. There's potential enough in here to free up a jammed highway, she thought, as the girl at the counter put it on a plate for her. The girl was dark and had large black eyes.

"Will you be coming here again?" she asked Freda. "Every fifth cup of coffee is free, if you have one of our coffee cards. They're for the regular customers."

"Then sign me up, because I'm sure to be regular after this."

The girl grabbed a pen and waited for her name.

"It's Freda MacDougall. M-A-C…"

"Freda will do. Here you go. Just get it punched every time you come."

I am a regular customer, thought Freda as she took a seat. Goodness me, one minute it's cloudy and looks like rain, the next the skies clear right off and you're feeling fine. The shop was smoky but relaxing; pieces of the *Vancouver Sun* were strewn on the tables. Freda read one of the many articles about the trial. The story was even bigger out here. Today they had a picture of him turning his head. He looked like a lost boy in search of his mother. She looked at the Corkie's crowd. Before coming in, she had noticed an acting school next door. Student actors were sitting beside her, talking about film class. She

DAVID DOUCETTE 🏵 67

had always loved movies and used to say to Milton that given half the chance, she could do a better job than many on the TV.

Freda finished the bit of coffee that was left in her cup. The muffin was gone, but she wanted to stretch out the morning as best she could. There was nowhere else to go yet....The article said they had found a glove covered with blood at the residence, which made him look really guilty now, but there were mountains of evidence to go through yet.

The actors left. The girl at the counter was wiping around the huge thermoses. She kept the place clean and organized; it was a pleasure to see.

"That's it for me," said Freda, standing. "Better get out before you throw me out." Brushing the crumbs from the table into her hand, she put them in the cup and took it to the counter.

"Thanks, Freda. See you tomorrow."

"Yes, I'll be here."

Outside the day was damp, the temperature near zero. The freezing humidity got inside the bones and lay there stubbornly. This indecisiveness is what's aggravating, thought Freda. Minus ten, minus twenty is fine, but if it's going to be warm, then let it warm up!

She made her way toward the library, steering well clear of Blade Park, as she had named it. She had been stupid, she knew this now, and would have to keep her wits about her in the future. Maybe it was a good thing that it happened.

"Savages," she said aloud.

"In the eyes of the Lord, we're all savages," a voice returned.

Freda turned to see a tall man with striking eyes, strong like vault doors. He had quickly come up behind and was almost on top of her. Clean and effeminate and looking past her, he appeared no threat.

"Savage, in the light of the Lord," he said.

Here we go, thought Freda. She turned away from him.

"Savage, till from the heavens, the angel Erebus floated down on a thin cloud proclaiming to all that the Lord Jesus reigns over all the legions of the living and the dead!" He moved on and was soon ahead. He had a Bible with him and was clutching it firmly in both hands. To others now, farther up the street, she could hear him delivering snippets of his sermon. He wore a flashy blue jacket and on the back was a marvellous depiction of Christ dying on the cross.

Walking along she came to a rundown telephone booth in which two young fellows, oily and wet like dogs, were pressed up against each other. The one only partially inside was getting a needle jabbed into his arm below a rolled up sleeve. "Get it in, get it in!" Freda heard him say. Oh, what an education this is, she thought.

Finally, she drew near the Roman columns. She was glad to know that she was getting true bearings, and could find her way to a few places now. In no time, she would be able to go anywhere here. I'll call Wilena later, she told herself, find out what bus I take to get there, or at least the streets I need to walk. I'll go over there today for a good old-fashion gab.

Pei-Jung was waiting, standing straight as a poker. Her big bag of books hung straight across her little shoulders, her thumbs through the straps at the front and her elbows tucked in neatly against her chest. She hurried towards Freda when she recognized her, smiling the whole way.

"Door not open!" she said. There were no lights on in the library. "You ready come to my house, very near to here. You know?"

"I told you about that, you know…Come on. Let's go."

She's all business, this one, thought Freda, and will have herself a million dollars in no time. Freda looked at the pair of slacks Pei-Jung was wearing; they were lime green. They might be all the rage back in China, thought Freda, but really! Even the ones with their earrings, scruffiness, and shaved heads must stare at her. I will have to get her a proper pair. When the time is right, I'll mention it to her and take her someplace to shop.

As they walked down Robson Street, Freda asked three times if the bag of books was too heavy. At first Pei-Jung only screwed up her face comically to brush off the concern, but then she became annoyed and so Freda kept quiet. Why is she so defensive? thought Freda. That terrible tone of hers, as if I committed some terrible crime!

"My house is Cardero Street. You know?"

"No, I don't know Pay. I don't know anything here, Pay. Vancouver is not my home! You got to stop asking me if I know things. I don't know if that's a Chinese thing, or what it is."

"Where your city?" said Pei-Jung.

"I have no city."

"You no have! Everyone have!" Pei-Jung looked up at Freda's face.

"Not me. I come from a little place, a village."

"Village?"

"Yes. On the east coast, six or seven hours by airplane."

"Waaa! Sixty-seven hours by plane! Canada is so hugeness!"

"Yes...hugeness. Come on."

"I think your home is the countryside, Freda. I think it's very beautiful at there. What is the name?"

"Ingonish."

"*English!*"

"Mostly."

They continued down Robson and Freda clarified for Pei-Jung the distance and the name of her home. They had been walking a long time. Pei-Jung began to apologize for the distance.

"It's all right. It's just that yesterday I overdid it and want to take it a little easier today. Let's just not go so fast." And she really did not mind. She had nice company and was getting to know her way around even better.

The pair turned off Robson and cut across a couple of other streets until they came to one called Davie.

"Wait, wait a sec!" Freda stopped. She reached into her purse and took out her eyeglasses and her address book.

"Yes sir! Look! This here is where my friend Wilena lives! Here, see, it says so here, nine hundred and forty, Davie Street. This is the same street, isn't it, Davie? There wouldn't be two."

Pei-Jung looked in the book, then squinting behind her eyeglasses looked up at the houses on the street. She seemed to have very bad eyesight.

"Your friend house here?" Her mouth stayed open; she was pointing at the house across the street.

"No, not here, but on this street. Her building is nine hundred and forty."

"That is other side."

"How do you know that?"

"This street, one, three, five, seven, you know? Other side is two, four, six."

"Oh, that's how it works? Pay, you know more than I do and this is not even your country."

Pei-Jung explained all cities were this way. She shook her head. "Freda, you must be from real countrysides." They laughed, then crossed to the other side of Davie and continued west until Freda could see English Bay and where she had walked around the Sea-wall the day before. She was about to mention it when Pei-Jung blurted out something.

"Ni hao ma?"

"What? Excuse yourself."

"Ni hao ma?" said Pei-Jung. "This is Chinese. How to say hello in Chinese. Yesterday you said you want learn."

"Did I? Give it to us again?"

"Ni, hao ma."

"Ni, hao *na*."

"Ma! Ma!"

"Take it easy, Pay! Jesus, you're excitable! Ni hao ma?"

"Good, good, you speak Chinese very well."

"Yes, I'm a wizard."

"But you must practice everyday. Practice. You know?"

They were continuing down Davie Street when Freda clutched Pei-Jung's arm, startling her. She said, "Here! Here! My friend's building. Look, see the statue of the boy pissing? I was here the other night!" She had her address book out again and confirmed the number.

"Come on, we'll go in for a visit!" She still had Pei-Jung by the arm and could feel the strain the books were placing on her little frame. They walked into the building and when they came to the big flat address board, Pei-Jung showed Freda how to find Wilena's name. Freda pressed the button. There was dialing, ringing, then a click.

"Hello. Heaven here. God speaking."

"You old crow! Let us in, it's Freda."

"Who's us?"

"I got a boyfriend. Open the door."

"Boyfriend, I don't doubt it. Here then, I'll buzz ya in." There was another click and Pei-Jung pulled the door when the lock opened.

*

As they walked inside the elevator Freda explained they were going to see her friend, who was from the same part of Canada, someone she used to play bingo with. Getting out of the elevator on the third floor and walking down the hallway, she and Pei-Jung shared the task of opening the fire doors. They went through the final one and Norman greeted them.

"Bring him back here, will one of yas?" Wilena called from her apartment. She was standing against the door casing as if she had never left. She held a burning cigarette in a cupped hand at her hip, near her medical bracelets. Pei-Jung called Norman to come, making queer low noises.

"Fat cat!" she said.

"Do cats get that big where you're from?" said Freda.

"So big, have not!"

When they reached Wilena's door, Norman tried running in but gave up after two or three steps and resumed his waddle.

"Ni hao ma!" said Freda to Wilena. "This here is Pay."

"Hello, Play," said Wilena, taking Pei-Jung's hand. Pei-Jung had no success with Wilena's name.

"I'm teaching Pay some English."

"And who's teaching you?" said Wilena and walked toward the kitchen, calling back, "Do you like tea, Play?"

"Pay! Pay!" said Freda. "Clean the shit out of your ears!"

"Oh, an expert on languages now! How about kiss my arse, translate that!"

Pei-Jung and Freda sat in the living room while Wilena was in the kitchen. There was the sound of a kettle on the stove heating up, and Freda could smell the cat box. Pei-Jung looked around the apartment.

Freda hollered, "Just tea, Wilena!"

"I checked into a room for ya," said Wilena. "It's right close to here and you can pay by the month. You'll be skint alive where you're at. Also, it's a hell of a lot safer here."

"Ah, for frig sakes, Wilena! What did ya go and do that for? I'm okay where I am!"

"Listen, Ranald! I went through the trouble of phoning all over hell's creation, so you take it! And let's talk no more about it, either; if it's a question of money, well then, we can ask Bobby."

"I still don't know how long I'll be staying, though, Wilena! You know that. I might be in Cape Breton next week for all anyone knows." Freda smiled at Pei-Jung. Pei-Jung smiled back.

"Why do you always have to be so difficult?" said Wilena coming out. "I know it's your nature, but I can use the company while you're here. The two of us can go over to that community centre they have on Denman Street. Bingo's every Tuesday night there. Young Play here can even come along with us. You and me will teach her how to take the jackpot home."

Pei-Jung sat politely, her posture smart. At well-placed intervals Freda smiled over at her, knowing full well that the little one had not the foggiest notion of what the two women were talking about. She looks afraid, thought Freda, and probably thinks we're fighting.

"You like bingo, Pay?" Freda said in a low, clear voice.

"Yes, I tell you that already. We play at school," Pei-Jung said.

"Oh, you do? Good then. You can come with Wilena and me sometime, all of us together."

"Together? Good!"

"Later though, not now. Another time."

Wilena called them to the kitchen. At the table they sat down to a plate of cookies and tea. Norman brushed up against their pant legs while Wilena told Pei-Jung about Cape Breton and explained that Freda was from down north. Freda made the mistake of introducing Pei-Jung as being from China, and was promptly reprimanded. Wilena laughed. The women had questions about Hong Kong. The women tried to familiarize Pei-Jung with the basics of cribbage. She had a lot of trouble counting her hands so they promised to show her another time. They all agreed to play bingo at the community centre the following Tuesday.

When Pei-Jung and Freda had finished their tea, they rose to leave. Wilena said a fond goodbye to Pei-Jung and invited her anytime, with or without Freda. Pei-Jung thanked her, and Freda said she would consider the room on Davie Street. On the elevator ride down Pei-Jung said that the community centre was beside her house.

"Your house? I see."

They continued until Cardero Street, where they took a right through the trees. Freda could see clearly again the waters of English Bay.

"That's where I was yesterday! It's called English Bay."

"Really? My Grandpapa always fish at there. You want to meet my Grandpapa? You want or not!"

Pei-Jung wanted a direct answer again. The weather had turned nice, and Freda said, "Let's go. But I'm not teaching you much English, Pay."

"No, is good. We can talking, so is good."

They walked back out to Davie Street and down to the water. Pei-Jung told Freda how her family had emigrated from Hong Kong only eight months earlier. Six came: grandfather, mother, father, elder brother, Pei-Jung, and baby sister, Mei-Mei. They had all come on the same flight, but the elder brother had continued on to Toronto to study English and to see what it was like there. The grandfather still had the family textile business in Hong Kong—an export enterprise of materials for women's clothing. In Canada, however, he had no business but spent his time fishing. Pei-Jung's father and mother had set up a small barbershop and convenience store: she cut hair in one room; he sold pop, chips, and lottery tickets in the other. Life in Canada was a struggle for the entire family, and everyone looked to Pei-Jung for English translation. It was she who had done all the paperwork for Canada Immigration. She had met with the lawyers and did all the talking when her parents bought their shop, and again when her grandfather had bought the big house in the British Properties in North Vancouver. She found the apartment on Cardero Street—her parents wanted to be close to their shop as they worked long hours. She also arranged schooling for her younger sister and herself. She complained in a mild way, though, in low tones. Recently, she had bought a new car for her grandfather. She had expected the sale to go easily, but it turned out to be surprisingly difficult—her grandfather was fussier than ever.

Everyone in Pei-Jung's family missed Hong Kong: the friends, the food, the shopping. Many of the Canadians at school were nice, but too busy to become friends. They were so young. Pei-Jung was twenty-one in high school. (Freda was shocked.) Pei-Jung seemed to think if she learned English fast enough and got into university, this might stop her family from talking about returning to Hong Kong. The Canadian lifestyle looked enjoyable enough: everything was so wide open here. Freda talked about herself, too. She had had two children, fourteen years apart, one was killed in a bad mining accident in Ontario. Vancouver was her first real trip, ever. Her husband worked on the golf course as a mower and died the fall before last. She didn't care for living alone, not one bit. She was happy she had come here, she said. Her life was simple and easy compared to what Pei-Jung and her family had been through.

"There's Grandpapa!" Pei-Jung called out, taking Freda's hand. The grandfather was reeling in his line, and when it was in all the way, he turned and stood straight for them. He smiled kindly. He took off his hat to wave it at them.

"This is my new friend," Pei-Jung said, then took a small step back. Freda stepped forward and shook hands. His was small, as well, but thick.

"I am Tet-Yin," he said. "Yin, okay? You are from Canada, huh. You like fishy, here, try, try!" He cast the line and passed the rod to Freda. The line was curved and heavy going down at an angle from the Seawall. She drew back on it a bit, but right away it felt as if the hook had snagged something.

"I haven't had a fishing rod in my hands since I don't know when!" she said and laughed. "I'm going to catch us one of those big salmon they got in the water out here! Watch me now!" She jerked the line and they all laughed. Freda heard Tet-Yin repeat 'salmon,' over and over. She looked at the two of them, granddaughter and grandfather, standing on the Seawall, both with keen attention and good posture. Tet-Yin was a round man, the top of his head as smooth as a baby's ass. His shoulders and legs were curved also, but his smile was nice. He must have been an attractive man in his day, thought Freda.

"Freda like fishy!" Tet-Yin came forward with his pail to show the perch he had caught. His laugh took on a squeal when Freda looked inside.

"Get those smelly things away! I'll get sick." She handed the rod back to him. He yanked on the line to bring it in but it really was stuck on the bottom. He drew the rod in toward his midsection and the line snapped. He reeled it in.

"Don't worry, I finished. We together go get coffee now."

Pei-Jung smiled at Freda happily and simply as if proud to have introduced a family member. Freda thought it all seemed a little rehearsed but then thought no more of it. They went to Tet-Yin's car, which was parked nearby. While he put his pail, rod, and tackle box in the trunk, Freda noticed that it was a fancy car. When they got in and he was behind the wheel, he suddenly looked very important.

They stopped at a place on Denman Street—the same shop where Freda had asked for directions to the library the day before. She said nothing about this. They sat at a table outside and Tet-Yin ordered the coffee, which caused some confusion. In the end, however, he made out all right; the coffee came. Tet-Yin and Pei-Jung waited till Freda had used the sugar and the cream.

"Freda, you not from Vancouver, huh? You visit here now," said Tet-Yin.

"How do you know all that? Yes, I am from the other side of the country."

Pei-Jung had her face turned to the street.

"The Atlantic Ocean," said Tet-Yin. "It's very beautiful at there."

"You've been there?"

"No, but I know."

Everyone sipped the coffee. The wind had picked up a little and brought with it the smell of rain.

"How do you like Canada?" asked Freda.

"Yes, sometimes it is cold. But I very like here, specially to fish."

Freda saw Pei-Jung check her watch.

"Pay here is teaching me Chinese. I'm teaching her English. She's a smart girl."

"No, I am bad student! Freda is good teacher and very kind woman. She has friend and we go to play bingo next week."

Freda encouraged Tet-Yin to join them, but Pei-Jung appeared to disapprove of this. Tet-Yin looked steadily at his granddaughter, as if waiting for permission. He said he could not go, then looked at his granddaughter and spoke Chinese. "I will go too," he said finally.

They finished their coffee and walked up to the the top of Denman Street. Pei-Jung showed them the community centre where the bingo game would be held. A small library was inside, near the entrance, and Freda led them there. Further inside was a skating rink. They went to see beginners twirl and fall on the ice. Pei-Jung and Tet-Yin looked on quietly.

The three of them promised they would go skating sometime, but Freda teased Tet-Yin for not being serious about it. He insisted he was. It had been many years since Freda had skated, but looking at these others move over the surface made her long for it. She recalled the lovely sensation of building up speed over ice, the long flat surface. Pei-Jung said she had to leave and Tet-Yin offered Freda a ride, but she declined. She said the walk would be better for her.

"Thank you very much for your teaching to Pei-Jung," said Tet-Yin as they were leaving the building. He whispered, "She have no friend here, she always study too hard. You know?"

The farewell at Tet-Yin's car felt as if they all would never see each other again. As quickly as the feeling came, though, it left. Freda looked back when the pair were in the car. Then, turning her head toward the sidewalk again, she moved away. That afternoon she moved over to Davie Street.

CHapteR 6

Freda's new spot was only a few doors down from Wilena's apartment building. Her room had a telephone, a small refrigerator, and a little stove. The area was much better; there was the community centre on Denman Street, English Bay, and the Seawall. The first thing she did when she arrived was settle down to a good nap. It was past six when she woke. She picked up the telephone and dialled Wilena.

"I'm coming over."

"Now, you're not going to start driving me crazy because you're alongside of me! Come on then. I'll fill the kettle. Oh, pick me up a book of matches on your way over. I searched this house inside and out and do you think I could find even one? I hate using the burner on the stove, it costs so frigging much. I want to light this little scented candle I have."

"Yes now, a candle, and how do you smoke them?"

"You'll find out if you don't hurry up!"

Wearing her best sweater and slacks, Freda took her lipstick out and dabbed some on her lower lip before working it all around. She tried to remember the last time she wore lipstick. It might have been for church the week before she left. On her knees by the bed, she said a quick decade of the rosary before putting on her coat and leaving. She felt stronger squeezing her new room key and putting it in her purse. She glanced back up at her new building from the sidewalk. Yes, it was definitely a step up.

A convenience store next door cast light onto the sidewalk. At the counter inside was a strong-looking man with a big gut. He had hair that was just too black, and a set of eyes to match. His shirt was wide open at the throat, revealing wiry hair that climbed to his neck. A gold chain, thick as a collar, hung in the hair, and around his wrists, gold bracelets.

"Got any matches?"

"Here you go. Cigarette, you want the cigarette, too?"

"I don't smoke."

"Then why you want the matches for? You gonna burn my house?" The man laughed out, his whole front shook. What's so funny? thought Freda. She picked up the matches and he did not charge her. Above him, on a shelf, was a small red TV. The trial was on.

"Who's winning?" she asked.

"Ha, ha. Winner, ha!"

Freda started to leave then turned.

"Okay, where's your house?" she said and winked, which caused the man's big front to ripple with his laughter, all his gold shining and shaking with it.

"I love to watch the flames when they go up," she said, lingering in the store. The man's eyes disappeared and he had to lean on the counter to hold himself up, he laughed so hard. When she finally did leave, he contained his hysterics long enough to say goodbye, but once outside she could hear him again. The nut, she thought, what kind of sociey must he have?

Wilena was out in the hallway when she got to her floor.

"Frosty out?"

"A little. No snow, though."

"Never snows out here. Come on in—you get my matches? I nearly set fire to the kitchen trying to get a light from the burner."

Freda was bending to take off her shoes. "I got them, but the foreign fellow who gave them to me was on drugs, I think."

"I don't doubt that a bit."

Hanging up her coat on the stand, which was already full, Freda sat on the chesterfield. The tea was ready.

"Foreigners," Wilena hollered out from the kitchen. "This place is chock-full."

"Don't I know it! Never seen the likes."

"Not many blacks, though."

"No? Why is that now?"

"Don't know. Perhaps I just don't see them." Wilena came back into the living room.

"That was the sweetest thing you brought here today. A little Chinese girl. Bright as a whip, too. All them Chinese are." Wilena came out of the bathroom and gestured for Freda to follow her into the kitchen. They sat at the table, where there was a fresh pot of tea.

"I met her at the library, up around the hotel. We walked down here, and right after, I met her grandfather down by the shore. The two of them have the exact same smile. You should see it."

"I'm sure that it's more than the smile. They all look alike."

"Not when you get to know them."

"Expert on races now too, are ya?" said Wilena, pouring the tea into the cups. Freda kept a little quiet, but was not upset by the remark. Wilena took out the cribbage board and slid open the metal drawer on the board's underside. Blue, red, and green plastic pegs spilled out over the table. Wilena chose the blue and green for the game; the reds she put back inside the compartment underneath. Freda won the cut for deal and started shuffling.

"Yes," she said. "I invited Pay's grandfather along to bingo with us next Tuesday. You don't mind. Yin is his name. We'll have a grand time. Should be a sight, too, he never played before."

"No! That type generally takes it all. Watch now and see if he don't go ahead and win the jackpot, leave us poor fools who's been making a career of it go home with not a black copper."

Wilena had a good first hand; she moved her peg twenty-one holes. Freda passed over the deck and Wilena shuffled in the standard way, lengthwise and, as usual, much longer than necessary. Freda reached for an Oreo and dipped it in her tea. Wilena stood up to put on some music after warning Freda not to start cheating by looking at her hand when her back was turned. There was a small cassette recorder on the top of the refrigerator.

"I know you're right crazy about this stuff, so I got Bobby to make me a tape. I don't mind it so much either, now, now that I'm out here. I listened to it this afternoon and enjoyed it. Here, listen...That's John Morris Rankin and those fingers are straight from heaven itself...Rita MacNeil was up at the Hudson Bay store the other day, signing autographs. The people out here really like her stuff. She was on the sixth floor. I didn't go because of all the rain; it was spilling from the heavens. She was just there for the lunch-hour anyhow."

"I'm getting to like her more and more," said Freda, who went on to tell Wilena about the time Rita MacNeil came to Ingonish, long before she was famous. "Milton didn't want to go in the hall because there was only a handful of cars outside when we drove up that night. Most of them were tourists. But I coaxed him, and we went. He was right, it was pretty empty inside, but we took a seat. Then the main attraction came out on stage and sang us a song. She came to the very centre of the stage, barefoot. A big straw hat was tilted on her head, covering half her face. Her voice was good and came out booming. There wasn't a crack in that old hall not filled with it. Her songs were about booze, drugs, and loneliness back then. She called herself a blues singer at that time. A little pack of local boys were in the back of the hall. They had got in free because they helped carry in her music gear. They were interrupting the show and talking in between songs, and Milton was going back and tell them to shut up. She was good that night; even back then she was something, in that little hall, with a handful of people. Going home, Milton said he was glad he went. He also said that we would never see her again because of the spectacle of her bare feet and the costume she had on. Also, all those songs about booze and drugs, how far could she go with that stuff? 'She doesn't play an instrument, doesn't dance, doesn't move. She only has a voice,' he said. But now look at her, signing autographs in Vancouver malls, songs on the radio, her music in all the record stores."

There was a knock on the door.

"I heard the music all the way down the hall," Bobby said coming into the kitchen. "Haven't started in on the rum yet, have yas?"

"That's for later when the sailors arrive!"

"Sailors? Oh boy, can I stay?" Bobby winked at his mother. She shot him a look back. He leaned against the refrigerator comfortably and ran a hand over his hair. Norman came out from under the table and brushed up against his leg. He looked down at the cat.

"For the love of God, enough Mom, what are ya feeding it? It'll soon lose the use of its legs. Take it to a fat farm or something. Get some birds for it to chase."

"I got enough birds in here right now."

"Perhaps you're fattening it up for the winter. It stinks, too."

"Shut up, will you, shut up! I'm concentrating here. I have enough work with all the cheating she's doing."

The card game was near the end. Freda sipped her tea and listened to Bobby and Wilena continue.

"…And I'm saying he's the only sensible one in this room!" said Wilena. "So what if he likes to eat? So what!"

"It isn't natural."

"And what's natural, Bobby? You?"

Freda pegged out, winning the game and not needing to count up her hand.

"See," said Wilena to Bobby. "You come in here and spoil all my concentration. You were probably giving her signals."

Bobby sat down and joined them. He and his mother continued to carry on, mostly on the topic of the card game. When Freda finally rose to leave for the night, Bobby suggested that he and Wilena come along and have a look at her new place.

Before long the three entered Freda's new building. She talked about the Granite Arch hotel, her room, and the other tenants who lived there. She told of the cockroaches, the gnome, the needles. She felt brave telling them what she had seen now that she was gone from the place.

Her room was on the third floor. She showed the place off— lifted the telephone receiver, switched on the TV, flicked through the channels. She opened the refrigerator, turned on one of the stove elements, and in the bathroom, she turned on the tap for the tub. Bobby and Wilena left after a few minutes; Freda listened to them go down the stairs. Back in her room she went to the telephone and dialled Nova Scotia. It was just after midnight Vancouver time.

"Hello," mumbled a stiff voice.

"It's your mother. No baby yet?"

"Jesus! Mom, it's the middle of the night!"

"It's earlier out here, just after twelve. I wanted to tell ya that everything is fine. I'm living next door to Wilena."

"That's good."

"No baby?"

"Nope, not yet. Just playing the waiting game. Your trip out good? Why the hell didn't you call us when you arrived? It'll soon be a week. People worry, you know."

"I know, there was just no proper phone till now. You know how bull headed I am."

"Jimmy said all your praying going down over Smokey made yas almost hit a deer on the north shore."

"You tell him that if my words did anything, they kept us from hitting it! Any snow?"

"We had a little yesterday but nothing serious, just a few inches. Altogether, there might be a foot down. They're having a really good year at the ski lodge, though. It's been cold and the snow-making machines go all night. You can hear them when you get up to go to the bathroom."

"How's the gang?"

"Everyone's good. Bradley keeps asking about you. Listen, Mom, this must be costing you a fortune. I'll let you go, but hang on till I get your number. Here's Jimmy."

There was the sound of throat clearing. "Where ya calling from, Freda? Jail?"

"Hi, Jimmy! How are you getting along?"

"Not too bad. Fired at a twelve-point buck the other day but he caught the bullet in his teeth and spit it right back out like it was a piece of chewing tobacco."

"Give me the phone," said Gloria. "I got a pen. Let her go."

"604-285-2783. I can't give you the address because I don't know it. I'll write it in a letter. I'm teaching English."

"I suppose! Okay, I'm going to let you go now. Everything is good here. Write the letter."

"I will."

Freda put down the phone, then washed, undressed and got down on the bed. She listened for the cars in the street. Everything is good now, she thought, drifting off.

*

The telephone rang early and hard the next morning. Freda immediately thought, It's Gloria! She's having her baby! Yanking the sheets away, she nearly tripped getting out of bed to answer the phone.

"Hello?"

"Norman's dead."

"Who? Ah, dear God, Wilena! You don't mean to say." A strange feeling came over Freda, as if this were the second time she heard this, as if she had already known what the call was going to be. Wilena was crying but her voice was very controlled, which added to the misery.

"I got up…He usually sleeps under my bed and gets up with me.

This morning I couldn't find him. He was under the kitchen table. I called him, I called for him to come out from under it."

Freda said she would be right over and listened till Wilena put down the receiver. She dressed in the slacks lying over the rail at the end of her bed, chose her red sweater then changed it for her blue. She washed her hands and looked over on the top of the small refrigerator at the bulb of garlic. Without stopping for her daily dose, she grabbed her coat and purse.

The streets were still dark. The sidewalk had a film of ice that made walking treacherous. Freda got in close, near the buildings, where it was better. She looked in the direction she was sure was east, but there was no sign of brightening. Although she was walking as quickly as she could, she seemed to be getting nowhere. Looking down, she realized she had no gloves on either, then imagined her wrists breaking in a fall. A car went by, the headlights made her freeze and squint.

She got hold of the railing at Wilena's building and stepped gingerly off the sidewalk. She buzzed, and Wilena let her in. The fire doors on Wilena's floor were noisy and seemed even heavier in the night, or morning—whatever the hell it was. Easy, she told herself, it's only a cat. What the hell was she doing with an old, obese cat anyway? Anyone could've seen it wouldn't be around much longer. She should have expected something like this to happen. Perhaps it'll teach her, wisen her up some. But her friend was not at her door, smoking, when Freda arrived. In fact, the door was soundly shut. Freda knocked lightly with her knuckle, then went in.

On the chesterfield, in the dark, sat Wilena. A light was coming from the bathroom and another light, a little one, came from the top of the stove in the kitchen. The second light did not quite reach her. Freda wished she'd found her smoking, doing something.

"Wilena?"

Freda stood in the middle of the floor, her coat and boots off. She suddenly felt very short. She sat alongside her friend and took her hand. The collar of her big coat curled up in her face, so she had to push it back down. Wilena's hand felt neither warm nor cold, and her face was grim as coal. Freda could see splashes of wetness at the corners of her eyes. Wilena's glasses were folded and on her lap.

"He was under the table, his four legs out. I thought he was stretching." Her voice broke off strangely and tumbled back down inside her.

"What can I do?"

Wilena made a puff of air, which sounded like a little light bulb breaking.

"He's in a Safeway bag in the kitchen. I don't know what I'm going to do with him. This miserable goddamn city; it doesn't feel any more familiar to me than it does to you. Where do you bury your animal when it's dead? They expect me to put him in a garbage bag, like everything else, send him to the dump and let him get mixed up with all the rusted cans and dirty diapers."

"I'll make us some tea. We'll do something, don't worry."

Freda went into the kitchen. She ran her hand along the wall, feeling for the light switch. When she turned it on, her eyes shrank in the light of it. So this is where the poor beast met his Maker, she thought, stepping in.

At least the smell has settled, she thought. Maybe it was Bobby's comments last night, that stuff about the cat being fat, that jinxed him and finished Norman off. But I made my share of comments, too. It wasn't only Bobby. Poor Wilena, always coming to the miserable thing's defense. Maybe the cat was able to sense all the jokes, took them to heart, and did itself in. Perhaps he had spent the night in despair, hauling his fat ass around from one room to another, trying to come to terms with what he had become. Perhaps he ate himself to death.

"I don't want any tea," Wilena called out. "Just come back in here and sit down."

Freda returned.

"Listen Wilena, I know it's a proper burial you want. I would, too. So how about if I look in the Yellow Pages and see if they have anything? They must have something somewhere here. If you aren't too fussy, though, I know this place nearby, and with it still being early, with no one around…I'm just saying that it would be more special than bringing anyone else into it. I'd be right there."

"Where? What are you talking about?"

"Down by the beach, English Bay. We'll do it high up, away from the water. It's sand there, the two of us could manage."

"What, and dig with our hands?"

"If we have to, it's sand! What we can't dig up with sticks, we'll use the hands God gave us. I don't imagine there's any real frost in the ground…It's what I would do."

Wilena shook off her faraway gaze, and stood up. "Come on then."

Freda asked if she could borrow a hat and gloves, then waited at the door. Good, she thought, grey light. She could see it out the living-room window.

"He's in a Safeway bag, under the sink," Wilena called from her room.

She wants *me* to get him. Christ almighty! Freda walked into the kitchen, bent down, and opened the door under the sink. There he was, encased in plastic, next to all the cleaning products. A heap of empty grocery bags was stacked around him cushioning his final nap.

"I'm going to double up the bags," Freda called out. "He looks to be a little heavy for just the one…To be on the safe side, I mean…"

She slipped the second bag around the cat and walked to the living room. Wilena was watching from the door, dressed to go. Freda put the cat down at the door and put on her boots.

The two set out and no words passed between them going down through the building to the outdoors. The bag was nearly too heavy for Freda to carry. She had to hold the fire doors open for Wilena, who shuffled in mourning, oblivious to the effort it caused her friend. On the sidewalk, Freda pointed her in the direction of

English Bay. The streets were just starting to come to life. The early morning weather that had covered this part of the city with ice remained cold and the sidewalks were still bad. The two women had to stop completely when two dirty city buses shot past, giving them a good dose of the raw cold. The ice crunched under their boots where they hit the sand or salt people had thrown down. Both kept their eyes down as they walked, scanning for untreated patches. The going was slow and Freda was suffering, having to shift the bag from one hand to the other; the plastic cut her fingers at the insides of her knuckles.

Then the first flake appeared. Freda was first to see it. She had not seen snow since Ingonish and was quietly very excited. Snow in Vancouver! Snow on the west side of Canada!

She fixed her gaze on the sidewalk again but would look up from time to time. It started to get heavy then, coming a little sideways. The flakes were big, frosty, and as they landed they softened everything. Buses, cars, and people were all made clean by it. But these flakes were large and would not last long. That's what Milton always said. Freda recalled him standing in his plaid shirt, leaning with his back to the heat of the wood stove and reaching over to the kitchen window to draw the curtains out of the way. He always predicted how long a snowfall would last—the size of the flakes told him everything he needed to know. He'd continue to look out, the curtains balled up in his hand. Freda was beside him in her memory of this, putting bread in the old stove or taking it out. The smell came to her now here on the sidewalk. She looked up as the snow lighted softly on her face.

They had reached the intersection near the water. Freda asked Wilena if she was cold. Wilena wore only a tam, a pretty green under the little pile of snow that had gathered on top. She looks much better out here in the air, thought Freda, but she should have put something around that throat.

"How heavy is this Jesus bag!" said Freda, looking to see how it would register. Wilena kept looking straight out into the traffic, and beyond, to the water. Was she always this small? Freda asked herself. She looks tiny in all this snow falling here in the big city. And old. Freda was about to say something further, but the light changed and she switched the bag over to her other arm.

The two crossed to the park and went down to the beach. The pavement on the way was black and wet. Freda held her head up. It was marvellous to watch the sky up above, where a shrunken sun was now up and trying to get out from behind the greyness. It was as still as an outdoor light with moths fluttering over its warm globe.

The beach lay ahead, white and barren. Freda asked to rest, and she put Norman down on a park bench, but kept her hands looped through the bags. Wilena's cheekbones were wet and her eyelashes held big drops. They started up again and were soon on the Seawall, heading in the direction of some bushes at the far end of the sand where the beach ended briefly. The women were making good progress when they stopped abruptly: someone had called out.

"Freda! Good morning!"

They turned and saw Tet-Yin. His complexion was ruddy in the snow, and a big stupid smile spread across his face. In his hands were his fishing rod and pail. He quickened his pace.

"Shit!" Freda looked at Wilena's face, but it told her nothing.

"Freda! You awake up early morning," Tet-Yin sang out.

"Hi, Yin. Yes, I am with my friend here."

"Hello." He looked at Wilena but knew right away something was wrong; his expression changed. He put his rod in the hand with the pail but did not shake hands with the new person. Freda looked down to see Norman's face pressed up firmly and visibly against the side of the bag—an eye, an ear, a lip curled in a perfect snarl up over the teeth and gums, clear as a photo through the bags. Freda tried to turn the whole thing around, but it was too heavy.

"Cat! Cat!" Tet-Yin sputtered like a fool, his eyes big circles. He pointed and quickly needed an explanation. Wilena said nothing and just as foolishly played the quiet friend at a chance meeting as if all this was the most natural thing in the world. Freda told Tet-Yin everything and his face contorted appropriately during the recounting. Cats, she thought. People and goddamn cats!

"Sand very frozen," he said. "I help, huh?"

He bent to place his rod and pail on the path, then went up over a bank and in behind some trees. He moved quickly for an older man, Freda observed. Perhaps the Chinese don't slow so much with age. He left shallow footprints where he walked, and was out of sight only a minute. Freda had just finished apologizing to Wilena when they saw him return. He was smiling and holding a silver shovel with a bright red handle over his head. Then he fell. Freda and Wilena gasped, but then neither could contain the laughter. He was down and not moving, but then he began to use the shovel to get up. His pants had slipped down some, and when he reached around to haul them up he started falling again. Once on flat ground he was all right.

Farther down along the path where it turned and came up again, the three left the trail and approached the bushes. The sand crunched under their feet. From one end to the other, the beach was a frozen desert, flat, white, quiet. The big cedar logs now looked locked in permanently. Tet-Yin found a very private spot near a log away from the tide. Freda laid the corpse in the snow, and with a branch, marked an X down to the soil. The snow continued to fall, and out in the bay the grey water seemed to swallow it.

Tet-Yin jabbed in his shovel, but the light tool did not make for easy digging. He had to use the corners to get the hole started. He was steady and confident. Wilena stared out at the bay where the flakes twisted in farewell dances as they lit on the water. Freda went and put her arm around Wilena and was struck by how narrow her friend's shoulders were. She had always thought Wilena was bigger than this. Neither spoke. They watched the snow on the bay and listened to the scraping of the shovel at work in the sand.

When the shovelling stopped, the women turned around. A hole about two feet long and the width of the shovel lay neatly before them. Tet-Yin had done a good job; it was clean, and he had piled all the sand he had dug in one spot. He was resting on the shovel, blinking at the snow that brushed his eyelashes. The women moved toward the hole.

Freda looked at Wilena, who nodded, then lowered the bundle down into the hole and let go.

"Take him out of the bags!"

Freda looked up. "Don't rush me."

"I said I don't want him that way! Take him out."

Tet-Yin laid the shovel on its side, and squatted quickly to help Freda bring the cat out. He was able to slide the bags back deftly and let the animal's own weight take it to the bottom. He balled up the bags quickly, making them disappear into his pocket in one odd motion. The grave was smaller with the animal in it, not so deep. Snow had already covered some of the turned-up sand. Freda closed an eye at Tet-Yin, and he understood; he was set to begin right away.

"A prayer first," said Freda, pressing her lips together, tilting her head a little to look at Wilena. "Our Father, who art in Heaven, hallowed be thy name..." She had opened her eyes near the end of the prayer to watch the other two. Tet-Yin kept his eyes closed, his head lowered into his neck. Wilena held hers up slightly, her face the colour of the edges of the up-turned soil.

Tet-Yin opened his eyes to discover both ladies staring at him. He stepped forward, raised his shovel and dashed a small load of sand into the grave. He paused, looking over at the women before continuing. Taking her by the shoulders, Freda walked Wilena toward the water again. Each load of sand made a thud as Yin worked. The sea water continued to gulp at the snow.

They turned to see Tet-Yin patting a wet mound. The women watched as he went in search of something. He came back carrying stones from the bushes. He was making a cairn, his hands getting dirty, wet, and cold as he worked. But it was a proper enough thing to do. Freda studied Wilena's face and was sure her friend approved. Then Tet-Yin, with shovel, fishing rod, and pail in hand, was ready to go.

When they reached the place where Tet-Yin had met them, both women thanked him. He started up over the bank to his car and they watched him go. Freda called out to remind him of the bingo game on Tuesday. But he did not turn around. She called up to him again when he was at the top of the bank but he moved out of sight.

"He handled the bank a bit better this time," said Wilena, and the two walked toward the traffic of Denman.

Freda took them to a coffee shop and bought muffins and coffee for breakfast. Wilena feebly offered to pay. It was still early and the shop was empty; they sat by a window. They left a wet trail on the shop floor and the water pooled under the table, but both felt better drinking the hot coffee. Wilena nibbled at her muffin. Everything will be all right, thought Freda, breaking the cap off hers.

On the way home, Wilena asked Freda to stay and eat lunch with her. Freda said she was meeting Pei-Jung at two but could stay till then, and once the lesson was over she could come right back.

Before they left Denman, they went into a shopping mall which was just opening for the day. They were not inside two minutes when they came upon a pet shop.

"Best cure there is," said Freda.

"All right then."

Inside the shop, they saw several kittens in a big pen. One was grey.

"Looks like a Howard to me," said Freda.

"He does, doesn't he."

The pet-shop girl put Howard in a small box with large round air holes. The kitten put its nose up through one hole and through the others he swatted his paws. They walked out of the shopping mall with Wilena carrying Howard in the box. He was so light, she was saying, like there was hardly any life in there at all. She said she was dying for a smoke but had forgotten to bring any. The snowfall was easing up and the sun reappeared, a small silver dime.

At her apartment, Wilena let Howard out of the box and he landed in the puddles of the women's boots. But he bounced right out of them to stagger sideways, flicking hard the water from his paws. He headed for the kitchen.

"There's a good sign," said Wilena. "He knows right where to go."

They took off their coats, and Freda followed Wilena into the kitchen.

"Let me open the window," said Freda. "That frigging tobacco of yours—it's enough to near make a person sick!"

"Go right ahead, if you can get it open. Be good to get some air in here."

Freda cleared some of the letters and spools of thread from the windowsill. She undid a brass clasp at the window's top and had to work at it a bit, but it came. Wilena set up the crib board and they started. The tea was good, the Oreos were good; best of all, though, was the open window. After a couple of games, Bobby came in.

"Do you two ever stop?" he said and looked at the kitten. "What's that, Norman's lunch for the day?"

"Shut your mouth!" said Wilena.

"What's wrong with you?"

"I'll have you know that we lost Norman last night. And you coming in here with your mouth again."

"What? He ran away?"

"No, he didn't run away! He died. I tried your door but you had already left for work. Freda here was good enough to come over. We buried him at the shore."

"Shore? What shore?"

"The Bering Strait! Where do you think?"

"Ah, Mom, I'm sorry. I didn't know."

"Yeah, well, you know now."

"And you two went right out and bought this here little fella?"

"Howard's his name," said Freda. They were all silent for a moment, the sound of the new name odd in the kitchen. Bobby shook his head and looked away. He joined the game, then, and they all drank tea. Bobby won three games in a row while the kitten explored his new home. Freda leaned back in her chair and for the first time noticed a painting of the Virgin Mary hanging over the refrigerator.

"Look at that now. The Virgin Mary, standing in front of that tree loaded with grapes. I never think of them having wine in those days."

"Wine!" Bobby said. "How do you think she got pregnant and didn't know it?"

"*Bobby!*" the women chanted but then could not contain themselves and the kitchen swelled with their laughter, sending poor Howard dashing to the living room for cover.

"We're going to burn in hell for this," said Freda, and this they found funniest of all.

CHAPTER 7

It was Tuesday night, and Freda was going to try her luck. Stepping out of her building, she looked up in the sky and told herself she was going to win. Bingo had been her outing in Ingonish. When she and Milton had been able to afford a decent car, they started making the trip to Sydney to play the bigger games for larger jackpots. She had met Wilena at one of these games. They had been late arriving because Milton had taken the car over to Speedy's on Commercial Street (not because they needed a new muffler, but because there was a sale on he couldn't pass up). By the time they got to the bingo hall in Whitney Pier, there were no seats left. The man was soon going to begin calling the numbers. People began to shush one another, as they readied their cards.

"You two! They're waiting for yas to sit down. Here, thur's a seat over here!" They turned and saw a small black woman, moving her winter coat off two empty chairs.

They got into the seats, and quickly prepared their cards and blotters. The bingo caller made the first call of the night and from that point in the hall came the pleasant sound of balls moving in their cage. The games were on. Freda whispered thank you to the woman, the first words she had ever spoken to a black person. In fact, she had never laid eyes on a black in Ingonish, even at the Keltic Lodge with all its American tourists around.

Where Milton and Freda sat that night the smoke was thick, but that did not matter, not with the intense concentration. Also, Freda knew that on this particular night she would win. She had had the luck with her all day and knew it, though she could not say anything because that always spoiled it, telling someone. She won a letter-H game and took two-hundred and fifty dollars as prize but kept very quiet about it. Milton only smiled. While the man who confirmed the numbers was checking Freda's card against the caller's numbers, the black woman turned around.

"Girlie, you got the luck tonight. Did you bring me some?"

"There might be still some in the car. You'll have to dig through the groceries to get it."

The woman smiled. "Yous two aren't from Sydney."

"No, we're up from Down North."

"Oh, yas're up from Down North! Up from Down North? Jesus, there's confusion. Don't mention that one to Santa Claus, or you'll screw him all up altogether, and we'll never get a present."

Bingo in Sydney became a regular event, and sure as anything they would run into Wilena. In no time she was saving them a seat and phoning in advance to report on the weather before Freda and Milton set off from Ingonish. She began each call by saying what the jackpot was.

But that was a while back now, Freda sighed to herself. Still, here we are together in Vancouver of all places, trying our luck again. And there's Wilena, standing in front of her building waiting for me, she thought, waving.

The women set out for Denman Street. Freda remarked that Wilena looked bound for the North Pole with the heavy coat, scarf, and big mittens she had on. They were both excited and Freda said that the feeling before the game was always the best, even better than winning.

"Better than winning? Don't be so foolish," said Wilena.

By the time they turned the corner onto Denman Street, they were very talkative. They made fun of the people passing on the streets. They likened everyone to someone else, to someone on TV, or people they both knew. Their remarks never flattered. Wilena asked to slow down at one point because she needed to catch her breath.

"It's only a quarter after seven," she said. "The game's not till eight. Leave the rushing to the young."

They saw a homeless woman then, about their age, outside a grocery store. She was arranging cardboard boxes the store had thrown out to make herself a bed for the night. They looked soberly at each other.

"I'll never get used to it," said Freda.

"No, me neither."

At seven-twenty they arrived and peered inside where the game would be. Two men were setting up the long tables. The hall was really a room, not at all big. It had green walls and a low ceiling with perforated tiles. It was the place, all right—Freda pointed to a small silver cage full of balls at the front. A small table with a microphone was next to the cage. No smoking signs were posted at regular intervals up and down the walls, and some people were trickling in to sit. They sat and gabbed, putting their arms across their breasts, an elbow up on the table. They kept their jackets on.

"I told you, bingo players are early people," said Freda. "They need to get the right seat, so let's ourselves get a table too before they're all taken."

"Get one close to the front so a person can hear the calls."

"What for? There's speakers all over the place. Anywhere will do."

They sat at the front below a speaker and hooked their jackets on the backs of their chairs. They looked around at the people gathering and started up again with their fun.

"Look there, Sampy Peters!"

"Old Milburn Whitely, look there!"

"And Stella Donovan, here, holding the prime minister's hand!"

Freda was better at the game; she knew more people, and was quicker.

A piece of panelling slid back from the wall and from behind it appeared the canteen where they sold the cards. Two older men were inside; one was selling chips and pop; the other was selling the cards. They were carrying on with each other.

They took their place in line for their cards and Freda kept an eye on the entrance, which had become a bottleneck with people trying to orient themselves. A few seniors were creating all the confusion. A group of them, who appeared to have come off the same bus, were unsure of what to do next. Mouths hung open for the sake of breathing, it seemed to Freda.

"There should be ambulance people working the doors," she said. "Back home I heard it said that bingo halls take more people than the wars ever did."

"I don't doubt it."

"Imagine that now, waking up in heaven and not knowing if you won the jackpot or not."

"Be a nice sight."

"I'd tell Saint Peter right away, 'Put me back, at least till I take it all. I'm set at the corners. You can come and get me after they call my numbers!'"

They were laughing when the man at the canteen asked how many cards they wanted. Wilena bought four.

"What are you doing with four?" said Freda. "Who's going to play them for ya—you're blinder than I don't know what."

"Freda. Kiss me arse, will ya," said Wilena, who walked away leaving Freda to deal with the expression on the face of the man selling the cards. He winked at his companion. Freda paid for four cards and a blotter. She caught up with Wilena and they walked to their table. They laid out their bingo cards before sitting and blotted the place marked "free" in the centre of each card.

"Don't tell me they let you two in here!"

They looked up from their cards, their noses crinkled like seals rising from ice.

"This is Jorge," Bobby said, introducing the man with him. "He's from Monterrey, Mexico." The fellow had dark skin and his hair was a like a big handful of steel wool. The women nodded at him, then to each other. He and Bobby took off their jackets, and put them on the backs of the chairs opposite the women. Freda told them where to go and what to buy at the canteen. Bobby said he remembered the procedure, and the women watched them leave. It was seven-fifty, ten minutes to go.

Wilena spoke up. "Where'd he find him?" she said.

"Who? This fellow from Mexico? What's wrong with him, he seems nice enough."

"I bet he jumped ship or something. And what kind of name is that, *Whore-hey*? Nice name to slap on a kid. How stoned were the parents when they came up with that one."

"Smarten up, Wilena. And don't start here, he looks all right."

"Yes, he's fine. God have mercy on my soul!"

Freda couldn't help it—she burst out laughing until tears came. Wilena jiggled and laughed, too. Freda looked around: she was in a bingo hall and with her friend. Then someone else was calling to her.

"Freda!"

It was Pei-Jung, and she had brought the whole family, all five of them! Tet-Yin was at the tail end. They all smiled, showing their teeth, the whole family looking fragile enough to break to pieces.

"Hello, Pay. Hello, Yin. You brought everyone!"

"Yes! Yes!"

"This is going to be a nice circus," Wilena whispered to Freda, who immediately got up and borrowed two empty chairs from a nearby table. Tet-Yin carried them over, and the arrangement concerning how the family would sit began. It had to be sorted out in Chinese; it seemed complex and important. When they were finally seated, they still had their jackets on and looked ready to run at any minute. Freda told Pei-Jung that they had to buy cards and blotters, and this was relayed to the family. They all stood up again, and moved toward the canteen. Freda got up and went with them.

At the canteen Pei-Jung took control and made sure everyone had one card and one blotter each. The bingo cage at the front was snapped on, and the balls started flying inside.The caller took his seat, and the first ball was soon in his hand. Freda looked up at him, waving her hand, signaling for him to wait a moment. He nodded. It was the same man who had been selling the pop and chips.

Pei-Jung's family returned to their seats, and everyone in the hall watched them as they anxiously got off their jackets and put them on their chairs. Pei-Jung had gone over the rules with her family in the car on the way to the centre, but she was going through it all again with her father. He raised his head for a moment, smiled at Freda and Wilena, then lowered it to concentrate on what his daughter was saying. Pei-Jung was slapping his hand whenever it came close to the card.

First call: "B-4."

"Bingo," whispered Freda, to those at her table. Pei-Jung, her family, and Jorge, looked up, confused and amazed, then dropped their gaze back to their cards when the next call came. Wilena was shaking her head and scanning her cards.

Glancing up from time to time, Freda thought the sight was marvellous. Jorge and Bobby sat opposite Wilena. Bobby kept an eye on what Jorge was doing. Opposite them was Pei-Jung's family. Her parents, across the table and down from Freda, had put their big, puffy jackets back on. They were quiet and methodical in their playing. The father would run his finger up and down the columns but not be able to locate a number. His wife would blot the numbers he had missed, while neglecting her own card. Mei-Mei, a younger version of Pei-Jung, sat beside Freda. She seemed to have much better listening skills than any of the others and was able to read the numbers fast. She wore glasses, and was done checking her card so quickly that Freda invited the little one to help find her numbers. Pei-Jung was on the other side of her young sister; Tet-Yin was opposite her. He giggled after each bingo call before focusing his eyes.

This annoyed Pei-Jung, and she had to constantly whisper to get him to stop.

Game after game went on like this. No one won anything, but everyone remained hopeful. Finally the jackpot was being called, and everyone grew very attentive; the numbers came fast, and the cards filled up quickly.

Then, "Bingo!"

The voice came from their table, but it had been uttered so quietly that only Freda knew that Mei-Mei had won.

"Louder! louder!" Freda and the others chanted. Pei-Jung nudged her. Then:

"BINGO!" the little one bellowed, rattling the next ball right out of the caller's hand. What a cry, tremendous, sailing clear up to the rafters of the room! The ball from the caller's hand bounced forward and dropped off the stage. He sat staring out at the audience with his mouth open like an old toad waiting for flies.

Everyone in the hall started clapping. They rose when they saw who was the winner. Delight shot up one side of the place and came down the other. Some at the back were getting up on their chairs to catch a glimpse of the little girl with the big cry. The card-checker came and took her card to the front of the stage but was having difficulty verifying the numbers with all the excitement. He had to get up on stage and check over the caller's shoulder.

Then he came back with the five-hundred dollars, which he presented to Mei-Mei. Her mother spoke to her, and Mei-Mei got up and stood out in the aisle. She was so slight, not even four feet off the floor. The applause grew louder, mixed with whistles and wails. Her family called to her. They wanted her to do something. She turned from them and stood still. Then she bowed for everyone, and had to reach up to catch her falling glasses. Even the caller was on his feet at the stage and clapping with his arms completely extended. Mei-Mei took her seat without smiling once during all of the attention. But she smiled now. She could not help it. She was looking up at her mother, who was clutching the puffy jacket of her husband's arm. The little girl was beautiful.

Everyone reached for their jacket and began to leave. Although it was nearly ten now, the gang at Freda's table decided to go for dessert. Tet-Yin suggested it; games always made him hungry, he said. Bobby mentioned a place nearby that served cheesecake. Freda and Wilena drove with Bobby and Jorge. Tet-Yin and family followed behind in their car.

In the back seat of the Datsun, Freda and Wilena sat slumped together. There were some boxes with cans of paint on one of the seats—to balance out the car on account of the bad springs. Bobby promised they would make it, but they would have to go slowly.

Wilena was first to start cracking jokes about the car, then Freda joined in. Jorge inspired them, laughing at everything they said. They spilled out of the car at the restaurant parking lot, still hooting and blind with mirth. Tet-Yin and his group rolled in and parked next to Bobby. They all entered the restaurant and two tables were put together. Mei-Mei ordered orange juice and the rest had coffee. Everyone was having cheesecake.

Jorge was now very talkative, telling everyone he came from a big Roman Catholic family of "seventeen or eighteen childrens." He said that when his mother was pregnant with the youngest, they had run out of names and were going to have to shoot the dog so they could use his name. They had to wait till the grandfather, who was very old and not so well, died—five years after the baby was born!

"Well, what was his name?" asked Wilena.

"Me! Jorge! I'm da beebee!" he shouted, turning his eyes large.

They all felt good. The coffee and cheesecake were delicious. When the party broke up, Freda and Wilena told Bobby that they would walk. They were on Thurlow Street and it wasn't so far. Bobby's car bucked out into the street and bounced to catch up to the rest of the traffic. Tet-Yin packed his troupe in his big car and sailed off next. The women walked up Thurlow and down Davie, promising that bingo would be a regular thing as long as Freda was here.

They parted at Wilena's building, and when Freda was a good piece up the sidewalk Wilena called out in the dark: "And for the love of God, Freda, leave the garlic alone!"

"You old crow! Fly to your perch before I come back there and fling you up there myself!" Freda listened for the entrance door to Wilena's building open and close.

When she was inside her own room, she felt that the day had been very good. But all days are good now, she thought. She washed and got into bed, reminding herself to write some letters in the morning and to meet Pei-Jung in the afternoon.

*

Freda was beginning to enjoy her new world; she had even grown slimmer. She knew now what to tell people who wanted to lose a few pounds: travel to a place far off, a place not easy to live in, and have a go at life there for a while. But do it alone. There is so much going on in the world, any place will do. Home, with its big kitchens and big refrigerators, make big people. The fewer the comforts, the better. Garlic helped. She was managing the raw, wet British Columbia winter with no signs of a cold yet.

It was Sunday afternoon and Freda was walking up Denman on her way to the community centre to skate with Pei-Jung and Tet-Yin. In the morning she had been to church with Wilena. The priest was from the Philippines and could speak fluent English—he had no problems at all with his "th." He told the congregation a joke about this woman who had been bragging about her son being a bishop. Everywhere he went, she said, he was addressed as Bishop. Another woman bettered this by saying that her son was a cardinal and was addressed as such everywhere he went. A third woman, who had stayed quiet, saw that the other two were looking at her.

'My son?' she said. 'Oh, he's just an ordinary construction worker. But he's quite good looking and, of course, muscular and tanned. When he walks through the door at parties everyone, especialy the girls, look at him and says, 'Jesus.'

The congregation cracked up, but then the priest began another story, a sombre one, about a beggar who had been diagnosed with cancer and was going to die. The priest knew the man personally and had spent time with him.

"He had more strength than what is common. He had no fear because to him the diagnosis had come as an invitation from God." This made Freda think of the blue-eyed homeless man with the German shepherd on Robson Street.

She approached the community centre. Tet-Yin was out front, alone, dressed in an expensive leather jacket with a fur collar. He looked nervous.

"Where's the little one?" asked Freda.

"Pei-Jung is not come today. She have too many homeworks."

"I see. Come on then, let's skate. I hope you can keep up with me. I'm good, you know."

They went inside and Freda talked about when she was a girl and how she could skate faster than the boys down on the harbour. "Answer me truthfully, can you skate?" she said. "I don't want you killing yourself."

"Can. There have many skating centres in my country."

The two had been alone before, but briefly. Tet-Yin paid for their skate rentals and they took a seat on a long bench. Because of his girth, Tet-Yin had a great deal of trouble getting on his skates. He could just barely reach his feet, and the new jacket only hindered him. Freda made him take off the outer layer of socks he had on. She pressed her finger against his laces and waited for him to swing his big arms down so he could tie them. He made pretty bows, but they were not nearly as tight as they could have been.

"I cannot skating now," he said. "Too tired!"

"I'll 'too tired' ya," she said. He's brave, she thought, coming out here like this, chancing broken bones! And what's this new jacket all about? It's brand new and meant for someone half his age. I'm sure he had the whole family out an entire day looking for it. What a sin. How strange that next to me on a rink bench, with his skates on loosely, sits a big, fashionable, Oriental cherub.

With the aid of the boards, he got up. And with Freda's help, he moved across the green outdoor carpet that led to a low door. Freda opened it halfway and looked out at the ice. Skaters whizzed by.

"You ready, big guy?"

"Am."

Opening the door wide, Freda stepped up onto the ice and pushed herself away from the boards to roll over tiny bumps on the surface. She breathed in the cool air. Skating...By God, how I love it! I'm going to come here all the time.

She skated to the very centre of the rink and turned to watch Tet-Yin make his debut. He was still at the door, holding on. People sped smoothly and steadily past him. He looked through them all and saw Freda, at centre ice, waving him on. She started to skate in to him, and then saw him go down. *Smash!* She tried to be serious, but the sight was so damn funny. He doesn't know how to frigging skate! I knew it, she said to herself, laughing all the way. She had to wait for some children to move around his body before she could get close.

"God almighty! You all right? I hope you didn't hurt yourself." He was on his side and not moving; he could not get up. More skaters skirted around him.

"I forgot skate," he wheezed.

"You forgot?" She gave him some help, but he was terribly heavy. When, at last, he was on his feet, his skates slid out from underneath him and, like a crate dropping from a truck, he fell again, this time taking Freda down with him.

"Get off me, Yin! I can't breathe. Are you trying kill us both?"

"I forgot skating."

"Yes, I'm sure you did. Get up!"

He was lying on his back, looking contentedly up at the steel rafters. But he was in the way of skaters. Freda told him to get the hell to the side by the boards. Rolling over, getting on his hands and knees, he made his way to the wall, explaining all the while how he wished he could remember how to do it. Freda followed him, to make sure the other skaters—all of whom he was oblivious to—would not run into him.

Once he was upright again, he reached around for the back of his pants and hiked up on them as best he could while holding the boards tightly with the other hand. But his legs wobbled and shook, and he went down one more time.

This time Freda really lost control and gave over completely to the comedy. She bent to her knees and stayed laughing. Then, going to him with tearful eyes, which she wiped with the back of her glove in order to see, she discovered he was on his side, his back to the boards. His face and eyes pointed toward centre ice, his head rested on an extended arm. He was talking to the frozen surface.

"I wish I remember, huh. I wish I not forget how to play skate."

Freda got him up. "Hold on this time, can't you, for Christ sakes!" she said, but she did not let him go.

Together they were able to move along the boards past the goal nets, where the high glass started. The other skaters had learned to keep their distance. He was determined, Freda gave him that. His aim was to get around that rink, and these skates were merely obstacles. Making one revolution was all that mattered to him. "Hey, big guy! You made of rubber?"

"Yes, I very rubber."

"But you're not hurt anywhere, are you?"

"No, I am rubber. Look, here's tire!" His free hand patted a protruding stomach through his jacket. His face had reddened and beads of sweat, large enough to drop, were at his eyebrows.

Freda stayed with him the rest of the way around the rink, but when she had him back to the door, she told him to stay put.

"You can go," he said looking tired. "I will not go this time." Carefully, he eased himself off the ice.

"You go, Freda," he called over the boards. "You go more skate...I am enough."

"No truer words ever spoken," she said, and skated off.

There were fewer people now. Tet-Yin had probably frightened them off, but Freda didn't care. Moving to where the skaters were taking corners, she began to travel clockwise around the ice, against the flow. She skated inside the others then turned to go with them for a few laps, keeping a watchful eye over Tet-Yin. She did not want him to conk out, the big cherub. He sat content, twisted outside the boards in order to watch her. She was ready to quit when she went round once more.

"You can skate very well," Yin said as she came in. "I like to watch you very much."

"I like to watch you, too. You need a little practice though, don't you think?"

"Yes, very need."

They took off their skates. Tet-Yin needed help with his laces, and sat still till he received it. He was not lazy; he was simply unable to undo them alone. They returned the skates and left the community centre. Freda was enjoying the wonderful electric feeling that always followed skating. Tet-Yin said he felt something electric too.

When they came to a coffee shop they went inside. Tet-Yin began talking about the fish he caught at the Seawall; he could not understand why Canadians did not fish from there. It was free, he said. He knew some guys that even used nets. All Canadians did was run, roller blade, walk around with their dogs—which also looked delicious, he said. Freda smiled but was too tired to respond.

"Must be quite the place where you're from," she said. "People all over the place. You fellas drive bikes everywhere, don't you?"

"No! Maybe in China have."

"But you're going back to China next year, aren't you? To your country, I mean? What's happening there, Yin?"

"Oh, Hong Kong is always China's country. But some Hong Kong people are afraid of China, huh? Many come here to Canada, that's why. Television and newspaper make people scared. You want to come to Hong Kong, Freda?"

"Kind of busy today I'm afraid."

"You want or not?"

"Take it easy, you and your granddaughter with your direct questions! Try asking things nicer than that. No, Yin, this is far as I ever wanted to go."

They finished their coffee and Tet-Yin stood up. When they made a move to go, he assumed the posture of someone about to give a speech. Thanking Freda for helping his granddaughter, he looked as though he might produce some money.

"Bu kerr chi," she said.

"Wha! You can speaking Chinese! It's wonderful." A big smile overwhelmed his face, making his eyes disappear.

"You want come to my house?" he asked. "I can cook fish for you."

"The fish you catch? You crazy?"

"No, I will buy the Granville Market. Fish fresh at there, have very well at there, huh. You know?"

Freda nodded and hummed in reply, having no idea what he was saying. Perhaps he's unlearning the language, she mused.

"You eat fish I cook, Freda? Want or not?"

"All right. As long as it is not from along the bay here, okay? Promise me now."

"You can coming to my house tomorrow. I am not so busy to-morrow. We can meet here. Is good idea?"

"Is good," she said. They parted in sunshine.

CHAPTER 8

As agreed, at two o'clock they were together again. Tet-Yin was standing by his car, which looked as though it had been washed. He was
wearing the same jacket from the skating session and held something in a cloth sack.

"Look, Freda. For you!" He drew back the top of the sack to show
the head of a salmon.

"Bleck! Get that dirty thing out of here. You think I want to see a
smelly old fish?"

He opened the car door for her. "What, are we getting married
next?" she said. But a slightly disturbed look crossed his face. "You're
quite the gentleman is what I mean." He laughed but had not understood. He started the car and they pulled away. The sky was grey,
and moisture hung close to the streets. Freda looked out the window.

"Every day is grey here, every damn day. I think someone takes
the sun and hides it in behind those big mountains." Freda thought a
little longer then realized it had been sunny only the afternoon before. "Maybe not all day, every day, but there isn't much sun, is there."

Tet-Yin did not respond. Normally he liked to prolong any topic,
and because of this, talking to him was easy. Making him out was a
different matter, but he was always responsive. "Everything all right,
big guy?"

"You want come to Hong Kong?"

"That again. You asked me that yesterday."

"But today I want you come to there. Next week is Chinese New Year. I must go to there for visit and check my business. We can go together. Not so bad idea, huh?"

"Yin! Go way with ya! I couldn't go there."

"I have special deal on plane ticket. You don't need pay." The traffic on the roads was not heavy, which was fortunate as Tet-Yin could hardly concentrate on driving. "Come to there, with me. Is good place, you must go before 1997, before China's people come. You can see my country."

"Yes, but I never travelled like that before. And I told you, this here is farther than I ever dreamed I would go in my life. And I made it, I'm here. I don't want to push my luck, you understand. Hong Kong—I don't even know which direction that's in."

"Same! Was same for me when I came here to Canada. I didn't know here."

"A passport—you need one of those. I don't have one. Can you even get one at my age?"

"Pei-Jung telephone the passport office yesterday. Five business days to get."

"What's going on here, a conspiracy? No! I'm sure it's too much money, Yin. I'm not even sure how long I am staying in Vancouver. Jesus, the things you put in a person's head."

"Money? This should never stop your travel. Especially travel with good friend. Open your eye, and listen to me, is good chance for you. But go or not, your choice."

They drove over the Lion's Gate Bridge, the same bridge Freda had passed when she first walked around Stanley Park. She tried looking down but could not see the park, let alone anyone walking in it.

When the car stopped they were in North Vancouver, in front of a stately home. This part of Vancouver was called the British Properties, Tet-Yin explained to Freda at the front door. He welcomed her inside and taking her coat, walked into another room while she sat down on one of two chesterfields in the very large living room.

The floors were wooden, polished, and slippery. Tet-Yin said he was going to the car. When he came in again, he went into the kitchen and asked Freda if she wanted something to drink.

"Got any tea?"

"Come here, see the kitchen."

She was amazed at the size of everything in the house, and by how clean it all was. Large stainless steel pots of various sizes hung by hooks inserted in the kitchen wall. Tet-Yin showed where the tea was and accepted Freda's offer to make it; he set to work preparing the fish. At the sink, he ran cold water down over the slit in the salmon.

"You must find the size of everything bigger here."

"Yes. Big. But how do you know if you not come to Hong Kong?"

"Listen, mister... Never mind. Where did you get the salmon? It's nice, pink."

"I go to the market at Granville. Is very good place but expensive. You know this house was Guiness family house? They built the Lion's Gate Bridge, you know? Everyone in the houses at here is very rich. I am the only Chinese here. The people here are England's country people, maybe. Rich."

"Why are you living here and not over with your family?"

"Investment." He had his sleeve rolled up now and was scaling the fish and cutting it. The backs of his hands were thick and bald but they handled the knife deftly.

"There was a family that made beer called Guiness," said Freda.

"Same family!"

"Yes, now? How do you know?" Freda looked around at the kitchen.

"You like that beer? I have Guiness beer here if you want to try. You want or not?"

"Want! But only if you'll join a lady." She got up and unplugged the kettle.

"You want ice?" he said.

"Ice in beer? Never heard of that before."

They shared a bottle while Tet-Yin prepared the meal. When it was ready, they sat at a small table in the kitchen. Freda enjoyed herself. The salmon was a bit raw and the spices nearly burned the head off her, but it felt really fine to be sitting and eating in a big place. She did not finish the whole meal but ate a lady's portion, as she called it.

After they'd eaten, Tet-Yin asked if she would stay a little longer to watch a video from Hong Kong. She could see all the big buildings, he said. He brought another beer and she allowed her glass to be filled, but promised herself she would not drink it.

They sat on a chesterfield in the living room and watched a movie with a Hong Kong star named Jackie Chan, a martial arts expert, who every other minute was chopping someone over the head. He was a major celebrity in Hong Kong, according to Tet-Yin, who wouldn't let Freda see much of the action because he kept pausing the video to give background on particular street scenes. The movie took the better part of the night. Neither Freda nor Tet-Yin had any idea what the story was about.

It was late, and only natural when Tet-Yin asked Freda to spend the night. She said she would stay on the couch, but he insisted on one of the many bedrooms until she agreed. Her room was next to his, and when they were both in their beds they began to talk through the open doors. Freda lay in the bed and breathed in the smell of the sheets and pillowcases. The bedding was either brand new, or very old and never used. Tet-Yin began a ghost story about a temple near his house in Kowloon. He asked Freda if she would ever sleep in a Chinese graveyard.

"You'll be sleeping in one if you don't shut up," said Freda. "Now close your mouth and go to sleep."

There was silence, then Tet-Yin said, "I am cold."

"Cold? You're over two hundred pounds and covered to the throat with blankets."

"Can I come there?"

"…Come on."

Tet-Yin climbed into the bed with her.

"But if I hear another peep out of you," said Freda, "you're getting your teeth to drink." She lay beside the big man, facing him, and he began laughing, which shook the bed. Freda figured it was happiness. After some silence and awkwardness, he moved closer to her. She didn't say anything and he touched her shoulder, then held her against him. Eventually she felt him hard against her, and, still on their sides, they became familiar with each other's bodies. It was a jabbing more than anything, Freda was thinking. People can jab each other if they want to. She was glad he didn't try to get on top of her to do it, though. Afterwards, Yin rolled over and lay on his back. There was nothing unnatural about this, thought Freda. She hoped it wouldn't come between their friendship though. Perhaps he'll go to sleep now, she thought.

In the morning, Freda finally had her tea. Tet-Yin cooked some eggs and made toast. The butter he used tasted strange. They left the house in search of the immigration office. Freda was getting a passport.

The place was downtown in a high building, but the office itself looked no different from any other government office Freda had ever been in. The take-a-number procedure was the same. When her turn came, she was instructed to go back and fill out an application from a stack lying on a table at the entrance. "Cursed old frig! Is a person expected to know everything automatically?" She took the application to a cubicle. It was complicated, too. Tet-Yin hovering above and looking over her shoulder aggravated her further.

"Go and sit the frig down! I got it, I got it!"

He went to one of the chairs at the side of the room, but she called him back.

"It says I have to get a priest or someone like that to sign this. I don't know anyone here. I told you it couldn't be done from here. And I need pictures, too. There's a lot to this."

They left the office and went out of the building. There was a photography shop across the street.

"Take a good one," said Freda, posing for the photographer, raising her chin and looking straight ahead. There were two flashes. Tet-Yin was looking at some camera equipment.

"Do you like cameras?" Freda had come over to him.

"Yes, I like, but not this price. Much more cheaper in my country."

Freda looked at the sunlight streaming through vertical blinds behind them. It hit in strips and he looked like a delicate, fat prisoner behind bright bars.

"You're always happy," she said.

"All my life," he said. "I am big, huh. Thin and beautiful people have many trouble, I think. Is true! When they get old they get sad. You think so?"

"Perhaps."

The pictures were ready, and Tet-Yin took out his wallet to pay. Freda protested mildly but knew that if he were going to pay for the trip, she had better get used to his wallet. It was a fat one, anyway, just like him.

There was still the problem of getting the passport application signed. On the back was a list of professions eligible.

"It says that the person should know you two years or more. And only these ones working in these big jobs can sign. What a bunch of foolishness! Wait now, one profession here is a pharmacist, and wasn't there a drugstore back across the street?" They went back across the street.

"I need a little help," said Freda to the young woman behind a counter. "I need to get a signature for a passport application. I know you don't know me from a hole in the wall, but I was wondering if you could do it."

The pharmacist was a tall red-head with devilishly pretty eyes, green. Freda noticed her name tag on her white coat and was going to joke about knowing her already, but then decided against it. It would be better to be serious this time.

The woman smiled. "You're right, I can sign, but what about this having to know you for two years? You just walked in the door!"

"Okay, well let's establish something then. Where are you from? We might know each other and never knew it."

"Nova Scotia," the girl said.

"There, see! I knew I could hear an accent. I thought it was Newfoundland. I'm from Nova Scotia, too. We're neighbours."

"Really, what part?"

"Cape Breton, Ingonish."

"For heaven sakes, I'm from Sydney! I guess you're right then; I have no choice. Are you here just passing through?…Freda, is it?"

"Yep. I am going to Hong Kong with this here fellow. It's my first trip out of the country. Vancouver was my first trip away from Cape Breton, but I guess my travelling days are not over and I'm moving on. Thanks a lot, I had no one here to sign it."

"Well, best of luck." The woman passed back the application.

"Well, thanks again." Freda paused then spoke up again. "You have lovely green eyes."

"I do? That's awful nice to say."

Tet-Yin stepped up to them.

"So, you're taking her to Hong Kong, are you? Better take care of her."

They let the woman get back to work and left the store. Freda explained where the pharmacist was from and why they had got on so well.

"I'm missing home, Yin. Is this really a good idea? You know my husband passed away not so long back and something like that takes a while."

"Yes," said Tet-Yin. "But maybe it important for you to go to there."

They walked to the elevators for the immigration office. She wanted to continue talking about whether it was a good idea inside the elevator but stopped and looked over. She was happy to have met him. He was good company, a good soul.

Back in the office, Freda submitted the application. The woman at the counter told her the passport would be ready in five working days. Tet-Yin said they could leave after they got it. They went out for sandwiches at a little spot just opposite Canada Place. Freda talked to Yin about when she first arrived in Vancouver, and then her husband. She could not believe how much she was saying and apologized.

"No, I like your speak," said Tet-Yin, and watched her as if she were a TV. She was excited about many things.

*

That week they fished along the Seawall, waiting for the passport to be ready. One afternoon they visited Wilena.

"How's that little ball of fur doing?" said Freda coming in the door with Tet-Yin smiling behind, trying to say hello. He had not seen Wilena since the bingo game, but Wilena knew all about him and Freda. Freda called after she had arrived home from his house. First the skating, and now salmon dinner, Wilena had said, then asked if they had slept together.

"That's for me to know, Wilena." Then Freda had explained that she was going to Hong Kong. "Jesus, Mary and Joseph—*Freda!* Are ya out of your mind altogether? You'll be kilt over there. And you'll go too, won't ya? Christ, are you trying to turn the whole world upside down?" But in Wilena's voice there had been something congratulatory, too.

"Howie's fine...aren't ya, How? He likes to bite and scratch a bit, though. Howie? Howie?" Wilena scooped the kitten up, set him in her arms. He jumped down as fast as he could and, landing on its feet, and scampered across the floor.

"Cursed old frig! He scratched me! Come back here so I can make mittens out of you! You two, take off your coats and stay a while, what?"

They walked into the kitchen, Freda brushing fluff from Tet-Yin's shoulders.

"Can't you keep your hands off him long enough to have a civilized visit at a person's house!" Wilena had on an old pair of glasses that magnified her eyes, making her look serious and deranged at the same time.

"I've got to make him presentable."

"No, you don't. We aren't in church here. Although it might not be such a bad idea for you to go to confession, Freda." They sat at the table. "So you two are going to Hong Kong. Where is that exactly, Yin?"

Freda laughed.

"What are you laughing at? An expert on world travel too, is it, along with everything else. Don't forget I was out here a long time before you, Missy, and probably will be long after you go."

"Take it easy, Wilena. Christ almighty, what's wrong with you? It was only that I asked him the same question. Don't get all up in arms. Just last night I asked him. He started to go on about China and Taiwan, but I got interested and kept cutting him off with questions whenever he was getting close to telling me. He mentioned Japan, and in the end he just said, Okay, okay, close to China. I still don't know where it is."

"Good for you! Doesn't mean the rest of us are that empty-headed. I got my reference points. I know where places are, and a whole lot better than you, I guarantee."

"Fair enough then! You ask him then. Fire away."

Wilena went into the living room and came back with a Reader's Digest world map. She passed it to Tet-Yin, who spread it out over the table. Freda moved papers back and all eyes were fixed on the map, everyone trying to find the country. Tet-Yin showed them the area but was having trouble because the map was labelled in English. When he did locate it, the two women had the top halves of their bodies on the table.

"It ain't the biggest place in the world!" said Wilena. "It's not much bigger than a speck of pepper, so how do they get all the people on it? The name alone is ten times the size of the place."

"It is very crowded, but Canada too big," said Tet-Yin.

Freda pointed out China, Taiwan, Japan, and Korea. She told Tet-Yin that she thought all these countries were a part of China. Wilena looked at him.

"Lord God, Freda, just look how far you'll be going! Right across to here, where will the plane come down and fill up?"

"It goes all the way, Yin—doesn't it?"

"Yes, no stop."

"How long does it take?" asked Freda. "My birthday's in the fall."

"Twelve hours from Vancouver." Tet-Yin had the map now. "But here is very far away, too," he said, pointing to Nova Scotia.

Wilena pointed out Sydney, then Ingonish, but there was no name written there. "Yin, see. Thur's a two-hour drive that separates us back home. But look, the island itself is three or four times that of Hong Kong. And look, we're right at the opposite ends of the world." All three looked.

"Why you two come to here?" asked Tet-Yin. "Must be beautiful at there?"

They looked at each other.

"Too frigging cold!" they said.

They put away the map and the cribbage board appeared. Freda had reviewed the basics of the game with Tet-Yin before arriving. He was slow, uncertain and a little anxious, as if he were involved in a game of high stakes. But he got the idea, and by the third game his pace picked up.

Bobby arrived with Jorge. Wilena had them pull out the table so they could get in behind while she made tea. Bobby sat on a stool that was too high for the table; Jorge sat on a low cabinet with a chesterfield cushion on it. Jorge, who just watched, was having Bobby explain the game to him.

"Where you live, Jin?" Jorge asked Tet-Yin.

There was a roar of laughter and Jorge looked over at Bobby. "Why you laugh! Oh, jes. Ju know where is his home, I don't think ju do!"

Tet-Yin's chest heaved as though it would come apart. Freda and Wilena raised their eyeglasses to wipe at their eyes. Bobby moved over to the stove and switched it off. The water for more tea had started to whistle.

*

They reached the airport quickly. Pei-Jung, Mei-Mei and their parents had come along. It was February, Chinese New Year, and the place was very busy with travelers heading to Asia. Tet-Yin had given his granddaughters scarlet envelopes with Chinese lettering upon arriving at the airport. He explained to Freda that there was money inside, that it was a New Year's custom for the Chinese.

"Don't take off yet!" It was Bobby and Wilena, Jorge, and Howard. Wilena was holding the cat by a long leash, which was dangling. The cat was getting caught up in it.

"Yas made it."

"Yes, we brought Howie," said Wilena. "I figured that since it was you who helped get him, I thought he might like to see you off as well as the rest of us."

"You must be excited, Freda," said Bobby.

They all took notice of Jorge then, who looked as if he were staring into the casket of a loved one, his eyes big as jar tops. Freda feared that any improper move or careless word would set him awash in tears.

"I guess congratulations are in order on the birth of your new granddaughter, Freda," said Bobby. "Mom told us about it on the way here in the car."

"Yes! It was right in the middle of yesterday's mad rush packing and getting things ready for the trip, when I got the call. My son-in-law Jimmy told me that Gloria was in labour, in the hospital in Neils Harbour. He called later in the evening to say it was a girl. They're calling her Freda Darlene."

"Not another one, don't tell me yas are carrying on the tradition," said Wilena. "Where'll this one end up? Trekking across the face of the moon?"

An announcement made over the speakers mentioned Freda and Tet-Yin's plane. Everyone hugged and whispered partings, except Jorge, who remained dumb. Tet-Yin's family was also silent.

Freda looked over her shoulder after she had gone through the metal detector. They were all still there, standing side by side like they were posing for some big, odd family portrait. She turned away and kept abreast of Tet-Yin. Neither one spoke on the way to the departure lounge, but when they reached the gate and found a seat, they relaxed.

"This will be something I won't soon forget," said Freda.

Tet-Yin smiled, and they looked at the others waiting for the plane. Everyone looked pleasantly tired. Aircraft were taking off beyond a big window. Freda discovered that watching them was like gazing into a wood fire. The planes were marvellous, great houses of steel, making their slow heaving thrusts into the air. Coming down was just as baffling—a rumbling, then screeching, and finally taxiing with the ease and grace of trotting racehorses. To think this is happening all over the world, thought Freda—this sliding down long flat runways, these sleepy cows lifting their bodies into the sky. It was as smart and common as falling rain.

She saw herself with Tet-Yin then, sitting inside a plane as the great thing broke into flames. The fire would be in the cockpit, in around the dials and controls and new computers. She tried not to but then went on to imagine two planes colliding outside the airport window in front of her. She could plainly see Tet-Yin jumping to his feet: "Oh, my God, Freda—look there! It's awful, huh!" Freda would pull him back to his seat, and hide in his big chest. He would wrap his arms around her, but she would still see the flames and hear the sizzling. Then, just minutes later, she and Tet-Yin would hear the announcement that their plane was ready for boarding. They would have to pass through the gate because they were instructed to do so and because other passengers were doing the same. At the threshold to the plane, she would catch a generous glimpse of the lines of stretchers moving would-be travellers, like herself....Freda imagined leaving Canada this way.

"Cathay Pacific flight number 225 for Hong Kong now ready for boarding. Would all passengers requiring assistance, or passengers with small children please report to gate 21 for immediate boarding."

"Our plane," said Tet-Yin. Following him to the boarding gate, Freda watched him as he put his airplane ticket through an electronic boarding-pass collector. The machine pulled the pass in, ran it through, then deposited it on the other side. Tet-Yin walked through and picked it up again. Without trouble Freda did the same, and they walked down the chute together to the plane.

*

Oh, this plane! Inside is huge, with leather seats, plenty of leg room...

"Excuse me, please" a young Chinese stewardess said. "Could I see your boarding pass? This is Business Class. You're Economy." Freda had been holding people up.

"All right," she said and went forward, looking for Tet-Yin. Economy had two aisles, and it was nine seats across. Freda moved down to Tet-Yin, who was hovering above their seats, removing his jacket. He opened the overhead bin and stashed the carry-on bags there. Freda gave him her suitcase and when everything was packed, he offered her the window seat.

The plane soon eased away from the terminal and began taxiing to the runway. Freda looked at the heavy wings outside her window. They bounced and looked horribly fragile.

Freda guessed that these huge planes never filled up. A few seats back a woman held a newborn in her arms. This could be something, Freda thought, but at least she's not right behind me with it. There was as an empty seat beside Tet-Yin and then the aisle. The passengers were mostly Chinese. Next to me, thought Freda, is the best of them.

"What's your last name anyway?" said Freda.

"What?"

"Your name? Your family name? I don't even know that."

"Lee."

The plane sped down the runway, and its nose rose off the Tarmac. The whole body of it shuddered, then lifted. Inside, the slanted passengers faced the plane's rising. Any higher, thought Freda, and this will be a rocket ship! She held on till they levelled out and she could hear the unsnapping of seatbelts.

Tet-Yin drank beer that the stewardess had brought by and became especially cheerful. Freda had a tiny checker board that Wilena had given them. The pieces were small and difficult to maneuver, and their magnets were no good, but they managed a game. Freda took over the conversation when she was able; a great summation of her life unfolded, but it was all fused together and the picture not so clear.

"Flying is making the two of us talk crazy," she said. "But it's wonderful to share my life story like this. It reminds me of when I used to go Christmas shopping in Sydney and I'd meet a stranger in the big lineups. We would talk about anything. Not even a minute would go by and we'd be sharing secrets and dreams. Our lives would not cross again, that was the reason for it. With strangers you always feel safe to talk about anything."

"Am I stranger?"

"I don't know an awful lot about you." She looked over but his eyes were shut. The beer had knocked him out. Then, feeling very sad all of a sudden, Freda turned and looked out at the wisps of cloud breaking over wing tips. They parted like smoke. Big mountains were far below. A group from a few rows behind were up out of their seats and looking down, too. Alaska was mentioned. It was a fine sunny day down there and Freda woke Tet-Yin to have a look with her. He pressed his weight up against her. The mountains were a rabbit-fur white, and terribly old and frosty looking. Not a settlement could be seen anywhere. There was just the silence, way, way down in wild terrain. Freda said a Hail Mary, her cheek pressed against the window, which felt nice and cool on her face.

"Okay, get off me, you big galoot," she said. "You had your look. Get up before a rib is crushed and my lung gets punctured. You'll squash the life out of me before I ever get to Hong Kong!"

A film began and with it came the pulling down of the window blinds. It suddenly got dark on board. Many people had already gone to sleep and were resting comfortably. Four hours and thirty minutes gone already! Back in Vancouver it was eight; in Cape Breton, midnight. From a small crack in her window, Freda peeked out at dazzling light, bright as the morning sun on a clear day. The sea in whitecaps was below now. It looked so cold and lonesome. Locating the sun, Freda eyed it a moment. On this day, the sun would not go down for her. She was chasing it, over land, over sea, leaving her world and gaining a day in the process.

Tet-Yin was sleeping fitfully. He wore a new blue shirt which, from the way his body rested, looked too small in some parts and too big in others. Freda shut her eyes and listened to the steady hollow gasping of the spooky engines outside, then fell asleep in the sky.

Drop.

She was awake. She had been asleep but had not forgotten the fact that they were hurtling through the air at six hundred miles an hour, above the chopping winter waters of some strange ocean.

Drop.

This time she came out of her seat six inches! She grabbed hold of her seatbelt and made moves to tie it together. She clipped it, then braced herself. Sweet Jesus, this is not good! She looked at Tet-Yin, who, sleeping like a baby, had his head laying comfortably to the side. A pair of boys in the seat across the aisles were playing cards and smiling.

Another drop, hard!

The seatbelt light came on. The boys' cards were jostled but they kept on. They smiled at one another. Dear Jesus, is no one feeling this but me? The pilot came on, speaking Chinese, saying a lot. Tet-Yin was still asleep but the jarring had at least opened his mouth. He looked like a Venus flytrap waiting for bugs. I should wake him…

Drop!

Drop!

"Get up! Get up!" Freda dug her nails in his arm. He woke and there were female voices now, protests, foreign. Freda shuddered. Still, the cursed card game went on. Businessmen had their seats drawn forward, their briefcases open. They were smoking cigarettes, though she was sure they were not allowed. They sat rigidly, counting all the money they had made recently, getting their affairs in order. Calm down, she told herself. She reached for Tet-Yin's hand when he was buckled in.

"Ladies and gentlemens, we are having some small turbulences now and ask that you fasten your seatbelts kindly."

Goddamn this, I don't even know who these people are, or where the Christ I am going! Are these the last words I am going to hear? Freda fought back panic.

"We are starting our approach for Hong Kong airport and will arrive in thirty minutes."

Oh, I'm worn out, worn…worn…out. Outside the sun, purple, the colour of Easter altar cloth, was low, almost setting. Pieces of cloud were quickly sliced and shot over the wing but then they absorbed the entire view outside the window. Tet-Yin asked Freda if she was fine.

The plane pressed down. The pilot said they would be landing in ten minutes. Getting out her prayer beads, Freda began an Our Father for strength. The stewardesses, buckled in for at least thirty minutes, were facing the passengers. The prayer beads grew warm. Outside the window the wing lights blinked in the darkness. Freda could then feel the ground coming up somewhere just below—like the final step taken on a dark staircase it came.

The plane started rattling and shaking, she dropped her beads. She could see lighted buildings directly down below the shifting cloud cover. She briefly imagined people inside eating their supper, there with their families. Come on, land, cursed old frig! Land! Land! Land! She pushed down on her feet and arse as if she could assist with the landing.

There was a terrifying blast at the back from the engines and the nose of the plane drew upward. Everyone cried out. Freda could see the runway lights just meters away, and they were abandoning them! The engines bellowed, and it was deafening. Slanted upward, barely climbing, everyone's head was pressed back into seats. Small tables rattled, armrests shook. The weight of the plane continued to haul them downward; Freda raised herself up out of the seat to help the plane get back in the air. Tet-Yin faced forward, unblinking.

This is too steep, thought Freda! The thing will fall back! The stupid pilot has aborted his landing and has the thing climbing like a tractor up a rope. It's too sharp, and this bastard will have it end here for everyone! The racket from the engines was making it impossible to think. Freda writhed in her seat, felt the belt dig in.

Then the mighty engines slowed. Better, better.

The card players, their game completely over now, sat buckled up and at attention. They looked to be strangers, as if a word had never passed between them. The businessmen had put the upright tables in position. The cries from the back died—everyone felt safer suddenly. There was an unnatural silence, even the babies were quiet. The plane was up again, level again. It was bright outside;

the sun was about to set. The plane began to circle in the sky high above the airport, like a ravaged shark in twilight waters.

There was a lengthy announcement in Chinese. Freda watched Tet-Yin's face. She had him by the arm. Then she heard the English and she told Tet-Yin to shut up.

"We are very sorry ladies and gentlemens. Eastern entrance has wind. We try the north approach this time … God bless us." There was a click, the announcement was over.

Dear God, are we in trouble here? Is this going to be it? He said God bless us.

The plane started its second descent, and with it the wails and cries resumed. Freda had her beads again and wished she did not have the pilot's words in her head. She reached for Tet-Yin's hand and was glad to have it. *God bless us*, why did I have to hear it? There was no need of it. But he didn't know the language and had made a mistake.

The plane came down through the cloud cover a second time. Everyone fell quiet as the mighty aircraft again began its rocking horror. Here we go, thought Freda, feeling briefly ashamed at her cowardice. She talked directly to God, something she rarely did, and thanked him for her life. Tet-Yin patted her hand and was looking ahead when the wheels of the landing gear cracked down heavily. There was a whistling and the wheels caught hold on the runway. A great furnace of afterburners came on, whipping reverse gusts and slowing down the plane almost immediately. Soon seat belts snapped and clicked, and people were on their feet, some wiping their eyes in their sleeves.

chapter 9

Freda thought she might throw up because of the reek of sweat from jammed bodies waiting around the luggage conveyor belt. After retrieving their bags, they had to wait a long time in line to pass through customs. When it came her turn, Freda put on as ill a face as she could for the benefit of the officer, who let her pass with few questions. She glanced at the stamp in her passport.

Tet-Yin had her arm and was pointing her toward a part of the crowd that held a sign. She narrowed her eyes and saw a long red banner which three skinny boys were stretching above their heads. WELLCOME TO HONG KONG, FREDA! Nice, she thought, smiling feebly. Tet-Yin wheeled their suitcases toward the banner.

About a dozen people, young and old, were assembled and beaming happily as if embarking on a journey of their own. When Tet-Yin and Freda reached them, their smiles deepened and everyone began speaking at once. They shot furtive glances at Freda, but she did not mind and was glad to be still for a moment. Tet-Yin began handing out red packets to the children, who thanked him with full reverence. They scrambled away from the crowd and turned to open the packets. They screamed at the money and thrust it above their heads. Then they lined up again in playful military style for Freda.

"I'm Song-Liu! Nice to meet you."

"I am Hai-Bo! Pleasure."

"I Tou-Yi! I am pleasure."

"I am Chun-Ann. Nice to meet your acquaintance."

The family knew that Tet-Yin and Freda were very tired, so they left the airport and headed toward a restaurant in downtown Kowloon. Freda listened to the children talk and point at the streets from the car. They seemed to be more excited than she was. In the restaurant they sat at one of many big round tables. On each table was a large wooden rotating platter. The idea was to take whatever you wanted as it came round. Freda said she was not so hungry, but in no way did that stop the family from piling saucy sections of chicken, pork and beef into their own bowls and immediately devouring them. They also tried filling hers, but she had to put her hand up in protest, saying she would try some soup instead. When she tasted this, however, a wave of nausea swept over her and she immediately lowered her spoon. The grandmother was looking at her, bobbing her ancient head, her smile short one upper tooth. She passed some rice to Freda, who was grateful.

The drive back was quiet. Bodies and faces too thick and too many to discriminate lined the route. Glimpses of short-sleeved shirts, flip-flops, purses, black hair drawn tightly behind heads were all Freda caught along the street, which was wet with humidity.

At the apartment building, a tiny elevator carried the family to their floor. Someone undid a multitude of locks at a cage outside an apartment entrance, through which the party passed into darkness. Freda could hear a lot of noise. It was traffic, coming in through the open windows. The apartment was on the twenty-eighth floor but it sounded as if they were on a midday street. Someone switched on a florescent light and Tet-Yin's daughter Mei-Fung went over to close the windows. Dead on her feet now, Freda could say little in the way of conversation and certainly could no longer joke about anything. Tet-Yin led her to a bedroom at the back of the apartment then left her. She immediately felt a surge of loneliness and wanted to call him back to her, but voices had started up in a remote room of the apartment.

The bed was strange, low, and hard. She could not sleep because it was too close to the floor. Also, there was a queer sour smell: mould, she thought, disease. She fell asleep for a while, but woke with a jerk and looked around, certain she was still on the plane. She listened for the cars and, touching the back of her hand to her head, she knew she was running a fever. Rolling across the bed and getting up out of it, she realized there was rubber underneath the bedding. It must be for the children, she thought. It was not disease she had smelled but chemicals, soap used to clean a pissy mattress.

The apartment was quiet; everyone had gone to bed. She heard snoring coming from the next room. She got up to check and saw Tet-Yin sleeping there, his mouth open the way it had been on the plane. Oh, to shut it all down like that wherever you are, thought Freda. It is a gift from God.

"Come on, Tets. Up. I need to use the bathroom."

His eyes opened. "This is Hong Kong," he said. "Did you have good sleep already?"

"Beautiful."

She was sitting on the bed beside him and felt stronger. "God, that plane ride here in the night…Scared the living Jesus out of me, but perhaps that was the intention."

"Zhoa ann, Freda," came from outside the room. It was Mei-Fung, who was half Freda's age but looked only as old as Pei-Jung, even at this early hour. The woman smiled and gestured for them to come and eat. Whispers came from other rooms, and so did crinkling sounds, the same that Freda had produced rolling off her bed.

Already there was a lineup for the bathroom: the three boys who had held the banner at the airport. Their brush cuts stood on end as if they were part of a science experiment. They were too sleepy to be playful now, but each smiled when Freda appeared. They wore smaller versions of the cotton shirt that Tet-Yin wore to sleep in.

"Freda, you first," the taller of the biggest two said. He reached out and held the others back, twisting his head in warning the way a criminal might among peers. She did have to go badly and was thankful; she found herself bowing. An older girl came out. Freda went in.

Inside the floor was made of small white porcelain tiles which went all the way up the walls to the ceiling. The floor was wet and Freda's feet were immediately soaked. A shower nozzle dangled and dripped below its clasp on the wall. High wooden sandals were by the door, but they looked too dangerous and too much work to put on. Otherwise, the place was empty, except for a very big plastic drum in the corner, which was filled to the top with water; a small pail with a handle was floating in it. She went back out.

"What kind of place is this? Where's the toilet?" she said into the kitchen, which was just outside the bathroom, she realized. It had filled with people.

"The toilet?" she said more quietly. "Where is it?"

The little boys understood, and they cracked up. They clutched their bony ribs and shook with giggles. The elders only looked on vacantly, until the laughter intensified and spread out to them. Tet-Yin stepped up into the bathroom, taking care first to insert his feet into the wooden sandals.

"This is Asian toilet," he said and walked over to a small hole in the floor. The entrance filled with the whole family; they were laughing, but also watching intently as Tet-Yin explained. The hole in the floor was solid porcelain, about a foot and a half long and about six inches deep. It had the appearance of a baptismal font. The little boys were above it, pushing each other, each quickly demonstrating how to squat and use it. Tet-Yin also gave instruction on how to bathe from the large drum.

"Get out!" said Freda. "I got it!" She shooed everyone and closed the door. She put on the wooden sandals Tet-Yin had worn.

The water on the floor had come from the girl's bathing. The big drum and pail were for dousing, the shower nozzle for rinsing off. So this is how they clean themselves, thought Freda—in the wide open. No walls, no curtains, just buck-naked in the middle of the floor with plenty of space. Pausing then to look back, making sure she had locked the door, she took the last few steps to the toilet. Unbuckling her pants and getting them down, bravely she got into position and used the toilet.

This is not so bad, she thought. Just a bit unsteady, but there is a bar in the wall to hold onto. You come in contact with nothing, and that makes it a hell of a lot more sanitary than the regular toilet. Nothing touching, nowhere—that is, if I am doing it right.

When she came out, everyone applauded. She told them she wanted to bring the toilet to Canada to sell. And if they weren't popular, she could change the for-sale sign from "squat toilet" to "bird bath." The family did not understand, but she felt she had to say something, as they were all clapping. What a challenge all this will be, she thought.

At the table, Freda was provided with a stool near the boys. The porridge was salty, hot, and smelt of burnt onions, but it was a lot better going down than anything had at the restaurant the night before. There was a pile of tiny fish in one bowl. The fish were smaller than minnow, and the family was eating them whole, eyes and all. Accepting a second bowl of the porridge, she noticed her fever had gone. She looked around. Everyone was pleasant here, enjoying their meal. She winked at the boys, and they winked right back.

*

After breakfast, Tet-Yin and Freda dressed for a day of shopping and sightseeing. Tet-Yin wanted to show Freda some of the waterfront of Kowloon, but cautioned that it was Chinese New Year, the greatest of the yearly festivals for the Chinese, and so the streets would be crowded.

They said good bye to everyone when they had their shoes on, the children dashing out to swing big happy waves at them, their arms like upside-down clock pendulums. Freda asked why they were not getting ready for school and was reminded of the holiday; they had risen early for her. Oh, she thought, remembering that the holiday was also why she was here.

Looking at her watch when they were in the elevator, she noted that it was twelve hours ahead here, and smack dab on the other side of the world. They walked out through a tightly covered passageway that led to a back exit. Tet-Yin put his hand on the bar of the door.

"Ready?" he said, looking at the expression on Freda's face.

"Bring it on."

He opened the door, and Freda immediately thought, Lord God almighty, how are we going to get out? They were met by a mass of bodies and profiles, like a single long creature with endless arms, legs, eyes, and ears.

"Let's go," Tet-Yin said. "Hong Kong is very busy." He took her hand; she held it lightly at first. There were two directions the sidewalk crowd moved in: out by the street, people went one way; next to the buildings, another. The sidewalk was like a big channel polluted with fish. Tet-Yin guided them in close by the buildings. Freda now had both hands on his, which was slick with sweat. Fall here and you'd never be heard tell of again, she told herself.

The crowd was far too much for her, and she was about to complain, when Tet-Yin broke from the street and led them down a sparse alleyway. She wanted to thank him but instead looked down at slimy water pooling in the cracks of the asphalt. It was suddenly dark here and smelled of pork, piss, and roasting chicken, mangy dog fur, and spicy chili sauce.

"I'm going to be sick."

"Just little more." Tet-Yin seemed to be more interested in remembering the way than he was in Freda's physical state. A smile spread over his face; he pointed as he moved. The alleyway was a path now, covered like a rain culvert. They were heading for the end of it, where there were large boxes in which people appeared to be living. At a break in the wall before they reached the boxes, Tet-Yin stooped to get through.

"Are we going to fit?"

"Yes, I come this way since I was a boy. Don't afraid, Freda. I know the way now." Before entering, she paused to look straight up, in search of some landmark, but all she could see were narrow walls rising from this slimy footing. She had no more bearing than a rat living in the sewers.

"All right, Yin, enough! Where the hell are you taking us? Am I going to be murdered down here?" He did not answer but pointed ahead to a grey light. The sound of a zoo or a forest started; a racket of bird calls echoed loudly on the walls of the passage.

"What's all this?"

Tet-Yin, stepping up out of the passage, could only turn back to assist Freda. They came out in the open air again, facing a strange market. The cacophony was indeed coming from birds that were strung up in cages above the elderly patrons. Then Tet-Yin, talkative once again, began to explain that it was a popular hobby to bring one's bird to breakfast in Hong Kong. This place was a coffee shop, he said. Here the owners had a chance to hear their birds sing outside, and all this screeching and screaming, wailing and whistling was a type of competition.

One especially old man who sat on the periphery of this great bird sing-off, nodded to Tet-Yin and Freda. They walked toward him. Tet-Yin and the man greeted each other. Freda smiled. The man was thin, wearing a loose V-neck cotton shirt. Wrinkles shot out every which way from a pair of bright watery eyes.

"Zhao ann," Freda said to him as they sat at his table. He had a toothless grin. Putting one thin bent leg up over the other, he rested his arm on his knee. He had a coin in one of his ears, and was eating rice broth, a short orange spoon lying in the mixture. Like a child, he either played with the food before eating or did not eat at all but put the spoon back in. Tet-Yin ordered the same from a rough looking man whose hair rose up like any one of the birds calling out above. The man pinched a short ravelled-up towel around his neck as he listened. His shirt was sleeveless and flip-flops protected his feet. He barked Tet-Yin's order back in confirmation then walked to a nearby table to clear away glass mugs.

The cages formed a black canopy over the patrons, who were old and dressed in pajama-like clothing. Some were playing checkers, others were smoking and watching the players. The beautifully carved cages looked to be made of sandalwood or rosewood.

"I bet I know what the speciality here is."

"Speciality?" said Tet-Yin.

"Do they eat any of the birds?"

"What kind you want?"

Freda hoped he was joking. The thin old man was eating at last, his movements slight but purposeful as he lifted the broth to his mouth.

"Freda, you like this place? Everyone brings a birdie here every day."

Above them sang the old man's bird. The cage was brass and weathered to a greenish tinge. His bird had a larger space to fly around in than many of the others, whose cages were newer, smaller. His bird made violent flashes of bright colour when it flew in short bursts.

"He say his birdie is twenty-two," said Tet-Yin.

"That right? I thought birds only lived a few years."

Tet-Yin related this to his friend, who paused in his eating to hear. He spoke at length this time, his eyes disappearing till he was done.

"He say all birdie here is very old. This is the place with all old ones and is famous in Hong Kong." Tet-Yin laughed and said something else to the old man, who was again holding his bent leg, his spoon abandoned in the food.

*

Later that afternoon, Freda and Tet-Yin found themselves at a ferry terminal in Kowloon. She had said a few times that the number of people in the shops and on the streets was really getting on her nerves.

"Where you want to go?" he said. "Bingo?"

"Look, I'm glad I'm here, but it's just a little too much all at once."

"No, I want to say we can play like bingo, play gamble, huh. We can go to Macau. You know there is famous gamble place, and not so many peoples at there."

They bought ferry tickets, walked aboard the *White Star* and took the boat across Hong Kong Bay to another group of ferries. Freda snapped pictures of No Spitting and Beware of Pickpocket signs.

Inside the terminal for Macau, there was an elderly British couple. They were talking to each other at one of several turnstiles leading to the ticket booths; they were hesitating about which to pass through.

"I don't know if I'm qualified to ask, but do you need help?" Freda asked. The man spoke, "Yes, we would very much like to discover where it is one should purchase the ticket to board. They keep changing these departure areas here." His head was bald like Tet-Yin's, but he had a nicely-kept moustache. He was thin at the chest and had falling shoulders.

"Come along with us. That's where we're headed."

"That's right good of you," said the man.

"Yes, thanks," said the woman with him. "We are grateful, it's not the easiest place in the world to get around." She was low to the ground and rather doughy; her smile revealed large teeth.

The four bought their tickets, boarded a nearly empty ship, and moved toward the back to a lounge area. They introduced themselves as the ferry began to yank backwards away from its berth. It moved out into waters of Hong Kong Bay, where it then swung itself around. Through thick plastic windows in the lounge, they watched tugboats and junks bobbing in choppy waters. Faster boats came pounding across the chop while these others were jostled in the wake.

The new companions were Gerald and Margaret Giraldy from Manchester, England. Their people were originally from Galway, Ireland. They, however, had spent their entire lives in England. He was an engineer and presently finishing a contract in Guangzhou, China, where he had helped build a nuclear reactor. A lot of construction was going on in South China now, he said. They were finally starting to do it the "right way." Communism was singing its swan song, he told them. Margaret, an X-ray technician, had not worked for the past year because of her knees. She did not expect to go back for some time yet, as lately her back had started acting up. They had one son. He was a louse. He had married a girl from Swindon but had been unable to hold her. He was now living in London; where exactly, they did not know. Last Christmas, he had called to say he wanted to get into the taxi business but would first need an automobile. Gerald had cut him off, but had wished him a Merry Christmas. He liked to borrow, they said.

The ferry was now in calmer water and there was almost no small watercraft. Freda told them how she and Tet-Yin had met, but Margaret was particularly interested in where Freda was from. The two women were soon chatting like sisters. Freda had everyone laughing with her impressions of the open market and the birds.

An hour and a half later, the ferry approached a small island. When it came to narrow waters, they could see a raised motorway spanning a wide bay on concrete pillar buttresses, which rose out of the water like giant arms. Gerald guessed that the structure was three miles long. He said it had been built to attract and impress, to draw new residents and visitors to the island.

Once the ferry docked, the four wandered up a long gangway the narrowness of which turned the few unloading passengers into a crowd. At the top of the gangway, a covered walkway was wide enough to be a part of a shopping mall. They walked up through the town and found a cathedral which, according to Gerald, had been bombed by the Japanese in 1940. All three sides along with the roof had been blown off cleanly. Only the façade remained, which was amazing, considering how complete the destruction of the other walls had been. It had once been a massive cathedral. People were milling about on the steps leading up to the façade as though waiting for mass. The four gazed up. Figures carved in stone, gargoyles, saints, and fowl gazed outward.

There was a fortress to see, too, Gerald said. Freda stayed by the cathedral and studied the gargoyles as the others moved on. These things had come from Old Testament times. They were so silent, so gruesome. Just under the pitch stood the figure of Saint Peter, gazing out over all creation, his long flowing beard touching the back of a rooster at his feet. All this must have inspired a little fear, thought Freda. She looked over at Tet-Yin, who had moved ahead. She went to him.

At the fortress were stately black cannons, and plaques that spoke of the protection the site once offered. The Portuguese had been here, and they built this fort with its guns pointing seaward. The four continued quietly, as if haunted. Freda looked out at the waters surrounding this part of Macau. I have travelled so far, she thought, and here is the ocean again, thousands and thousands of miles from home.

CHAPTER 10

Beautiful faded greens, blues, and reds decorated the windows and doors of the older tenement houses of Macau's streets. Gerald explained that the architecture was not Asian, but European—Portuguese in particular—with its common French traces. One of the buildings looked like a restaurant. The four stepped inside. Macaroni was on the menu, and the few customers were filling themselves with it. The group ordered four bowls, and Freda sensed that Tet-Yin was not so fond of this dish but was being kind and forgiving to the simple palates of his company. The bowls came with big spoons already inserted. Ladling up the noodles, they began to eat while the other patrons gazed at them.

"This is not a Chinese dish," said Freda.

"Originally it is," said Gerald. "All pastas are. They have their origins here in China. It was the Europeans, specifically the Italians, who were first to take the Chinese noodle and make it famous worldwide. It was a discovery in their eastern travels to establish trade routes. The man here, of course, is Marco Polo, without whom the discovery of China and their noodle would have been delayed somewhat. We have the Portuguese, who colonized this particular real estate, returning what had been taken. Macaroni in Macau, a Chinese dish by way of Italy. Is there nothing you Canadians know?"

"We know they call that kind of talk pompous, and people who use it, pommies." Freda looked Gerald in the eye. He was blushing, as if he had been caught before an audience with his fly down and his shirt-tail out through it. Margaret slapped her doughy knee.

"That's the stuff, Freda. Tell him!"

"Ha! Yes, that is spirit," said Gerald right after her. "I like it. Put her there, Freda, you're quite something else." He had his hand out. Freda took it and squeezed hard. Gerald's smile quivered at the ends near his silver moustache. Tet-Yin did not know how to respond, the exchange had come so quickly, but he was proud because he knew Freda had in some way put down the Englishman.

The four came to a small crowd outside a shop. It was a celebration for the opening of a new restaurant, as Tet-Yin explained. A band of young men was donning the head, midsection, and tail of a dragon costume. Others were erecting small platforms which looked like little sawhorses and would act as props for the dragon.

A rapid banging of metal started, and the red papier-mâché dragon with its six denim legs began to sway. It raised then dropped its head. Movement shuddered down its body and flicked from the tail. The dragon's large eyelids fluttered like a coquette's and were oddly in sync with the other gyrations. People moved back to give the dragon its needed room. Freda thought the dragon and its movements were marvellous.

Gerald went forward, twisting the lens of his expensive-looking camera and snapping a quick picture. He stood in the way of the show! What an ass he's making of himself, thought Freda. All he wants is attention for himself.

A sulfurous smell and the sizzle of ignited wick was coming from a length of clustered firecrackers, which hung from the top of the restaurant's doorway down to the street level. Shots rang out. Tet-Yin pulled the ladies back. The three held their ears while keeping their eyes on the performance.

The dragon, crazed by this further stimulus, rushed in and out of the firecracker smoke, the music now fiercely loud and much faster. Gerald, still restricting the dragon's performance, had his camera poised. Some firecrackers exploded and a piece struck him as he squatted to snap a picture. Falling, his camera dangling, he immediately clutched the upper part of his face. He approached the others slowly, cupping his eye and forehead.

"Bloody natives and their ceremonies!" He turned to Tet-Yin. "Nothing personal, old boy, but I took a hit and have suffered a wound. No stretcher needed, though. No alarm, no alarm. Defective firecrackers. They sell them all along this peninsula, and this sort of thing is to be expected."

He removed his hand so they could see. There was no blood or no cut, but half a left eyebrow was gone and in its place a fresh redness bloomed. He blinked at them and the brow looked like a shrunken, frightened caterpillar.

"What a mess!" said Margaret.

"What?" said Gerald.

"You're eyebrow, dear! It's been blown off."

Freda turned to face the dragon again so she could laugh freely.

When the festivities had subsided, the four moved on. Gerald turned out to be a good sport after all, laughing and smiling at the jokes the women made of him. Still, the others avoided looking at him directly.

They entered a casino next, and Gerald started to explain that gambling was precisely what Macau was famous for. The smoke and the noise made the women complain. Also, Freda saw that Tet-Yin looked tired under the bright lights; she knew that being with a group of tourists had to be exhausting for him. She took him by the arm.

They walked the long distance back to the ferry terminal, where there was a McDonald's restaurant. The place was empty and from their seats, they saw that it had grown very dark outside.

"The quick nights here have to do with the proximity to the equator," explained Gerald.

"Is there nothing you don't know?" said Freda.

"Is there *anything* I don't know, you mean?"

"No, what I mean is—what's it like being such an ass, Gerald?"

He shrugged his shoulders and they waited for the ferry in silence.

Although the evening air felt warm and wet, the breeze over the ferry brought a pleasant sensation to the skin. The men went inside and came back with beer for everyone. They decided on the outside deck for the return trip. The plastic tables and chairs were smooth and cool, and everything was bolted down.

When they were out on the open water, they could see the lights from little islands and from the coast. The wind tossed and twirled the women's hair. Margaret grabbed a handful and held it to the side of her neck. The ferry was moving at full commuter speed and everyone was looking at the dark outlines of the islands. Smoothly rounded, these islands looked like cut-out shapes. Most of the lights shining in past the islands, however, were from houses in China.

"That's the mother over there," said Gerald. "And how clearly I remember my first trip on her. A few moons back, I dare say, but her song still comes to me on the decks here. You were back home in the UK, Maggie, all alone. You had just got out of hospital, re-member, when I had to leave. It was my first trip for this business of the nuclear plant in Guanghou. The company initially sent me to Hong Kong for preliminary meetings. But I remember having a few hours to myself one particular afternoon, when I get it in my head to take the train up to the mother. Yes, China, right off in there, look.

"I had heard about it all my life, but like most of the world—rather most in the outside world—had never been. But it was simply a matter of making the decision, of getting aboard the train and riding up to the border, which is what most things are in life, a matter of making the decision. Or so I thought.

"There's a town called Shenzhen there, not all that far, really. To prepare, I dressed myself down, in old clothes, you know, protection and all that.

"The train reaches its last stop. I alight with the many others who are arriving with their precious cargo of caged chickens and turkeys, and between their own language and the sounds of these animals, the station becomes like a regular barnyard...No offence, Yin fellow, you understand, it does get a little noisy. One woman I see has a crow in a box. Yes! You could see it past the wooden lattice. The fate of this particular winged creature I refused to imagine. I look up, instead, at the building that meets the station—Immigration. Beyond this are two round sooty hills quieter than the moon—my first glimpse of the great empire. I could smell sewage from the start, the very same odour filled my nose when, as a boy, I put my foot through the rotten sewage cover in the field below the family house. I had been dashing through the long grass when I did it. My nose was full of this same smell, though I was long gone from boyhood and far from home. I turn to watch the train leaving, going fast in reverse, leaving me in the hands of Fortune at the Chinese border.

"I proceed through a series of corridors then through a few queues; I go up a set of stairs and right back down again. I go and do God knows whatever else there is to get into the country. A Communist nation, understand; there's always a lot of rigmarole to getting in, a whole complex of buildings you have to pass through—Customs, Immigration, Fruit and Plant Inspection. What the hell have I brought on myself, I'm thinking! I only want to get in for a few hours! Signs are everywhere. One in bold red print says, No Cameras! I can still smell the sewage. I didn't want any trouble, though, so the disposable camera I had with me I threw in the first trash can I found.

"I don't really know how but in the end I have in my hand a day visa for the place. So next I'm walking down a corridor wide enough to spin an eighteen-wheel lorry in. I can hear my footsteps as, suddenly, there is no one around me. Then I see all these skinny Communist police coming forward, with heavy rifles over their shoulders and fingers looped in around the triggers. Any second I expect a bullet to come and wing me in the shoulder.

"I realize soon enough that this place permits the foreigners their entry. That's why no one is here, but, dear, they had built it expecting legions. But enough of that, I made it through to China, and what a sight it was!

"The largeness of it all is what I recall mostly...this grand pavilion they had built outside Customs, walled in at the sides and no less than a dozen football pitches in span—fields, I guess you call them in America. Bloody Americans and their poor usage of English."

"Shut your stupid mouth and give us a break for once," said Freda. "That better usage?"

"Yeah, well..."

"But don't stop," said Freda. "As I don't suppose you could if you tried."

"I will ignore that, and yes, I will go on...You should have seen the pavement! It was awash in a sea of bodies. By Christ, the entire population had come out to greet me. I get to the shops at some length, well into Shenzhen now. I look down and see a dirty pair of shoes, my own. All dirt roads here, you see, in this town. And everywhere is an old woman out on her blanket, selling two, three worthless items she has laid out on the road.

"Bicycles and cars are going by. Flat tires—in use! Other bikes have bent rims, missing spokes. Taxis, the same. One rolls past with a flat tire and a beat-out window. All this going on in common daylight. But is all this a question of being poor? No! It simply has to do with not fixing things, simple things. But the people, that was the worst, all walking around with the spirit bone-dried out of them."

"Those damned eyes....The first and final thing this accursed Communism takes, the spirit, the heart. It spins out a society of ghosts.

"I find myself at a river. The strange thing about it, though, is that it's dead. Yeah, a dead river! Ever seen one? I hadn't. There is water in it, but it is as still as rusting metal and just as colourful. I look up and realize the sky is identical, brown from pollution. Rubbish was floating in this river. Nothing recent, rather stuff dropped by previous generations and never picked out. In the streets is the same, rubbish tossed down and too much much work for these ghosts to muster up the ambition to pick a piece or two of it up."

"Jesus. You live with this," said Freda to Margaret. Gerald stopped, turned his head toward the wind and stared out at the darkness, then drank his beer. But the others were quiet, and no one could deny wanting him to go on, to end it at least.

"Enough of that, though...I'll settle it up. But is any of this bothering you Tet-Yin?"

"It is what you see," said Tet-Yin.

"So here I am walking the dirt streets of a border town when one, then two men begin to follow me, which is the whole point of all this, my story. Initially, I suppose they have nothing better to do, but they have at least that much imagination in them to be curious about a foreigner. I look at them. They're wearing white short-sleeve shirts. Skinny, the pair of them. They stop, pretend to be hanging around when they see me looking. So I start off again, slowly this time. I decide to get more bodies around me, which is no great feat considering where I am. So going into a busier area, a street with loads of these women sitting out on their blankets, I reach the real commercial zone. I look back first, then squat beside one of the women—when there is opportunity to bend my knees, that is. And I have to squat, too, because she isn't going to stand. No, too comfortable on the ground!

"I look at her wares. The same that was by the river—junk, all of it. A couple of stained jade Buddha pendants but the rest worthless. Since I am down here, however, looking over her items, I guess I am participating in a sale now. People stop. There are two pieces of stone, milky-coloured, of absolutely no value. They had my eye, though. To this day, I don't know why. They were the size and shape of small eggs, smooth. Sounded like glass when they clicked against each other. I suppose I wanted them. They felt good in my hand.

"But the certainty of the woman then! Yes, the sale was all wrapped up—a foreigner on her blanket, money in the bank. We tried to communicate a price but I would have had more success deciding the dollar value of something with the black crow back at the station. God blind me! I am only down in the dirt with her to escape these fellows and a fine job that is, because everyone in the street is on top of me now!

"She's rattling away in Chinese, playing with a vamp's smile, a natural seller with nothing to sell, eyes turning in, lips lifted. Isn't this wonderful? I got two worthless rocks in my hand, and two guys following me. I expect to feel a knife enter at the bottom of my neck at any moment. But there's comfort in the notion that this jab won't be unhindered, not with with half the country pressed up against me.

"Enough, I want to move on! Let me out! But the only thing I can think of is to show her the contents of my wallet, to allow her to choose a bill to complete the sale. I'm getting cleverer all the time, because once I get my wallet out is when the real pressure comes. The rabble, they descend on me like birds on bread. I'm surrounded, elbows jabbing in against my sides, bodies foul, and stinking every-where. They are peering into this wallet that I, a regular buffoon, have open on a street in China! They are all trying to get a good look. The ghosts have come to life for a peek. It was awful. This is all I am here, a purse. But I hold fast, because what is inside is mine. The notion of this gives me strength somehow. But the thing is, it's only travelling money I have on me. But what is travel money for one might be two years of food or frivolous shopping for another.

"The seller is now up on her bowed legs pointing at what I have broken open, pointing at the largest bill, mind you, while all around me is heated breath. Of course, all I have are Hong Kong bills, and I don't know one from the other. In the end, she takes something. Or

I give it. I don't know. Whichever it is, I throw it, crumbled up, feeling ill as hell with having been cheated so well. Stones in one hand, I clamp shut that stupid wallet and have to be very forceful to break away. I push, I swear, spit, do everything I can to get through. A harrowing moment, I don't mind telling any of you."

He stopped and lifted his bottle. The others were looking at fixed points in the dark. The ferry rose, fell. Everyone tried to appear nonchalant but each one had been very much listening.

"Get me back to the order of Hong Kong is what I'm thinking. Imagine that for a moment. See, see how the mind works? Nothing meant by any of this, you understand, Yin, about Hong Kong I mean. Hong Kong is top notch on my list.

"At last, the vast pavillion and beyond that Customs. I thank the Lord above, the end is in sight. I climb this overhead walkway that's hanging above a long line of taxis, which look as if they haven't moved in years, when a girl approaches me. A young girl, thin, a beggar of not more than eight or nine years old. She sees me and walks boldly and blankly over and takes my hand, dirt at the corners of her mouth, eyes unblinking, innocent as a moment yet as old as time itself.

"What's this? I'm thinking, when she extends her free hand to expose the palm. She's looking for change. Blast! Right after the woman sells me the rocks, I get this. Be gone you wretched little urchin! Leave off! The thing is, of course, even if I had it in my heart to give her a coin, I knew full well that there were scores just like her waiting in the shadows, hiding in under this walkway. One glimpse of a shiny copper and I knew I'd have them all over me like crabs over sand. But she won't let go of my cursed hand!

"Then the singing starts. Yeah, this Chinese song starts up from her, her little lips humming and pursed like a carp's. It sounds old, but her voice is quite lovely, actually, haunting. Everyone is looking now. But what else is new, my whole day has been a spectacle! We're walking along together, the two of us, hand in hand, pretty sight!

Now, a drunken bloke, a railing missus—these I can handle—but walking with someone's little Chinese daughter across this stage, I'm at an utter loss. I really am! But I can only go along with it.

"Then she's making for my pocket, and I push her hand clear. She's pushing her luck too far. But blast—that cursed tune, over and over, so spooky and it's starting to become familiar. But she won't let bloody-well off! All kinds are stopped now, old and young, watching, and she's pinching me, feeling around with her dirty little hands at my pockets, and all the while looking right up at me with big childish eyes.

"She's got me good, pinching at my trousers—here, right here at this right front one. Well, you know what happens next? Of course, she clamps down on the glass stones I've just bought. She doesn't know, though, what they are. Then she—it'll be with me forever— she looks up to acknowledge that she comprehends what she's found, and strike me down if there isn't some sort of consent in those eyes of hers! Ah, Lord, Christ, something broke off inside me. I yanked my hand away, tore it free; I take the hat off my head, and throw it down before her. 'There!' I holler right at her. 'You want something! Take it! Go on, it's yours, take it and nothing else, you evil little Christer!' Well, her eyes grow round like pinwheels and her tune stops. And that ended my day."

The boat was in Hong Kong waters. The lit surroundings looked like a magical forest. Freda took over the silence and directed everyone to the sight of the city at night, the activity still on the bay. She watched Tet-Yin and could not detect his mood. Even at night, the smaller boats were tearing from every angle across the water. As the ferry got closer, the water became a state of dark steady confusion.

*

Most everyone was asleep at the apartment when Freda and Tet-Yin returned. The three boys were cuddled up on a leather couch

watching the news on television. Mei-Fung appeared in the light of
the TV, looking sleepy. She tapped the boys on the cheeks and directed them towards the toilet. They staggered along, their bodies
rigid, poorly coordinated. Tet-Yin and Freda sat at the dining table
and were served cola and cake, which was not very sweet. Freda
watched Tet-Yin talk to his daughter. One boy after another mar-
shalled past on his way to bed, but each managed a smile and a
good night for Freda.

That night Freda slept poorly; the time change had finally hit
her. She lay on the bed, tossing about, and the squeaky sound of
the rubber sheets made her want to tear them off. The stillness in
the apartment kept her from getting up. Her mind turned first to
Cape Breton, then to Vancouver; both were her home now, it
seemed. She found herself longing for the Seawall and remembered her first trip around it. She recalled the bill of Smokey, too,
and the geography of the two places mixed like cut-outs in her
imagination: Cape Smokey was on the other side of English Bay,
Canada Place overlooked Ingonish Island. Lion's Gate Bridge was
the Seal Island Bridge on the way to Sydney. It was all a little mo-
saic, little landscapes that flowed together seamlessly. Strange and
right. However, she knew Hong Kong could never get mixed up in
any of this. No. Just the same, she would love to remember it.
Eventually she slept, smiling.

Freda regretted having promised to meet Gerald and Margaret
the following evening. Tet-Yin was busy, but he wanted Freda to go
if she wanted to. When the day was going well she said she would,
and even though she had had enough of Gerald by the end of last
night, Freda was not going to stand anyone up in Hong Kong. She
went to the underground station nearest the *White Star* ferry terminal in Kowloon, where the couple was waiting for her.

When they reached the bar, Freda relaxed. The place was filled with
dishevelled characters from all walks of life. Mostly white, the patrons were noisy and robust. Mad Dog's of Kowloon was the name of

the bar, and Freda wondered if the name had brought the characters or the characters had brought the name. Gerald ordered three doubles. "They're having a special," he said.

Margaret looked at Freda and winked happily. They sipped their drinks, then remembered to clink them.

"Well, what about yous two? Where did you go today?"

"We took our lunch at a restaurant over in Hong Kong," said Margaret. "At this place on the beach. Two Scottish sisters were working there."

"Big hulking things," said Gerald. "It's good you weren't with us."

"They were working their way around the world, they told us."

"Eating their way around, more bloody likely!"

"But they looked the travelling type, I must say. You know, awfully tired looking," said Margaret.

"As a result of the sexual part of their appetites, perhaps."

"Gerald!" said Margaret. "You're getting too familiar here."

"But that's a good thing, isn't it? It shows that we're at ease in Freda's company, yeah?"

They ordered more drinks. Gerald and Margaret talked about life in Manchester and how the local pub made society great. It was the place where people properly learned how to discuss issues of real importance; it was the basis for civilization. Just then a British sailor broke into their little talk and introduced himself as Martin.

"Anyone got a fag?" They said no, but he seemed more interested in a chat than a cigarette. He asked everyone who they were and where they were from. When it came Freda's turn, she apologized to him, saying she could not make him out; and since he got so little from her, he kept his eye on her. He pronounced his "th" as an "f." He talked about himself some, about his family in Manchester, and a grand-aunt from Manchester who visited at Christmas and always smelled of piss. He and the other kids held a scrap before her visit to see who would sit beside her. He talked about the good beer in Manchester, then left.

"Is that your civilization?" asked Freda after he had gone.

"Not quite," said Gerald. "Believe it or not, though, he lives only down the road from Maggie and me, not more than half an hour. But even I had trouble following him!"

The music got turned up and everywhere voices were raised in conversation. The three drank and talked a great deal. When it came time to leave, they pointed out to one another that there was a great number of empty glasses at their table. Margaret could not walk.

Gerald tossed her right arm up over his shoulders and held her around the waist. Freda got round to Margaret's other side when there was space near the doorway.

"Forgive me," Margaret said.

"Yes, forgive her," said Gerald, past the lolling of her head. "She rarely gets like this, but she so very much likes you, Freda. We both do."

"Yeah, well, you should be a lot nicer to her. I don't know if it's an English thing but you've got a big mouth."

"I do?" said Margaret. "Forgive me for that, too." Freda and Gerald smirked and Margaret threw up. They stopped to let her retch.

"Get it all out," Freda said. "Finish it off."

She did. Then pausing, she looked up and said, "I guess I've had a little too much."

The hotel was not far, but it took them over an hour to reach it. Strangely, taking a taxi did not occur to anyone. The hotel room had two beds. How English, thought Freda, as she watched Gerald sway as he tenderly took off his wife's coat and shoes, and helped her to the bed. Gerald pulled the bedding up around her neck.

Before Gerald and Freda went out the door, Margaret stretched one long arm up perfectly straight in the air. She mumbled between her teeth, which now appeared much larger than before.

"All the best, Freda," she called out.

Then the arm went limp. Gerald took Freda to the elevator. Having cared for Margaret seemed to loosen up some of the alcohol held back in his brain. Freda noticed how much he was swaying now that he no longer had Margaret to support. When the elevator doors closed, he slurred, "Ah, Freda, you're aces!" then leaned into her and began kissing sloppily at the corners of her mouth. He had her backed up, but she just let him. She had been in the situation before. Besides, it was not totally unenjoyable.

*

Freda spent the following days with Tet-Yin, wandering around the city, eating, and getting her bearings. When they were together, the time went so well. She liked this. Every morning he was up early and waiting for her and always had a good day planned. She knew he had a business agenda while in Hong Kong, and although she told him to do what he had to, he was still good enough to show her around.

One morning he took her to his shop, which was a private little place with bolts of material for dresses stacked horizontally to the ceiling. He showed her what made good material. He really knew about colours and cuts of clothing. Freda had never even considered how a garment was cut, but he said shape and design were in the cutting and it was a very important thing. His daughter and son-in-law were there. All four sat down to noodles in behind the textile bolts, near the office desk. When Freda dropped her chopsticks on the floor, they got her a fork.

On their last night in Hong Kong Freda and Tet-Yin went to the Peak, a look-off that rose steeply out of the business district. A cable-operated train, which climbed like a worm up a tree, carried people there. At the top were circular shelters which had obviously been a part of military defences for the harbour. The smell of rain hung in the air here, and a group of tourists all wearing white hats were investigating the area. They spoke in a language that Freda thought was not Chinese but something more quiet, secretive.

"They're Japanese," said Tet-Yin. "Since I was a boy, I always see them up here." He followed Freda over to the shelter's edge after she took his hand for support. They looked down at the view of Hong Kong far below.

"They must be raising the air temperature with those lights...It's a beautiful place, Yin. You must be proud of it." The boats in the harbour and bay were agleam, and the water looked as still as any of the buildings. She turned to watch his profile. "Really, thanks for this. You've made me a happy woman, and I'll not forget any of it."

He was not looking at her. "You want food?" he said, then indicated the restaurant they had passed on the way to the shelters. Many windows overlooked the night view and inside were many Chinese with Western table-mates.

"I'm not so hungry," said Freda. "And we only just ate a couple of hours ago."

"I am hungry. Tonight, we will have good Hong Kong food. You want?"

They went in, took a table, and were served like king and queen. The dishes arrived in small delicate bowls. So far, Freda had managed without chopsticks, but she had received private tutelage from Tet-Yin's three grandsons for the past two nights; they'd had a wonderful time at it. Now she was at least not afraid to try them, and Tet-Yin complimented her. In truth, she was dropping food all over the place, but some of it was getting in her mouth. She stopped after a few minutes and ordered coffee. Tet-Yin continued eating alone, which appeared to be fine with him.

Freda asked about how the British got to be here, what would happen when the Chinese marched back in. She was looking through the window when she spoke, pointing to where she thought the mainland was.

"It will be same in Hong Kong when the Chinese come, I hope," Tet-Yin was saying. "I talk to many people on this visit and no one is so afraid. China's people not so bad. But people here was at first very scared. Some maybe still." He twisted his head and went back to his food. A hearty eater, at times it looked as if he could not be filled. His family was like this too, even the girls. Freda drank her coffee and her eyes went again to the scene below.

"Freda," he said, pushing his last little plate away. "This is for you. Take it please." He had pulled a small box from the pocket of his shirt while she had been staring out the window, and he slid it towards her. A ring was inside.

"What the hell's this?"

"Don't upset," he said. "It's for you. You know?"

"Oh, I see. Yes, I guess I do know. I didn't think it was done this way." The china clinked as the waiters cleared tables. Freda reached her hand across and touched Tet-Yin's forearm above his watch. The chopsticks were still in his hand. The waiters came and collected their dishes. Tet-Yin told them in English he was satisfied.

CHAPTER 11

Twenty-four hours later, they were in Vancouver. Wilena and Bobby were waiting with Pei-Jung and her family. Mei-Mei was holding Howard in her arms.

"Your cat looks as though it has gained a pound or two already," said Freda coming to them. "You, on the other hand, look as though you lost a bit."

"For Christ sakes, what's all this! She wasn't even gone a week and listen to her!"

"I was away nine days."

"Well, it takes a little longer than nine days for the world to change."

"I don't know about that."

"Why? What's it now? I suppose you're moving there." The group was moving across the airport floor, where much of the inside traffic was being diverted due to construction of a new terminal. They kept getting separated as they neared the exit. "Look!" said Wilena. "Look what's on her finger! Don't tell me that's what it's supposed to be! Is it?"

"It is, he asked and we're going to. He gave it to me at a place called the Peak."

"I bet he did...Let's have a look." They gathered around. Everyone said it was nice, but nothing else.

"You work faster than Red River Cereal," said Wilena and kissed her friend. The others in the group followed with hugs, but there was a heavy silence. Howard was over Mei-Mei's shoulder, holding on and blinking. When they finally parted company, Freda gave Tet-Yin a kiss and said she would call him later. She held his hand.

"Leave him go," said Wilena. "Didn't you have your fill in China?"

"Shut up, it was Hong Kong, and did you ever know a woman to get her fill?"

"Yes, I did."

The parties climbed into their respective cars and drove downtown. Bobby spoke up as he was driving, asking Freda about the trip.

"It was all great. The food took some getting used to, but the people were grand. What I need right now, though, is my bed. I'm played right out. Where's Jorge?"

"He's got himself a few problems with Immigration that he has to take care of. He's looking at deportment if he doesn't get things straightened out."

"Oh dear. Why?"

"Lord knows."

They dropped Freda off at her place. "I'll come over for a game of cards if it's still early when I wake up," she said.

"I'm happy for you, dear," said Wilena. "Just don't get any notion into that head of yours to be moving over there. They'll all blame me back in Cape Breton. Besides, there's no bingo there."

"Don't worry, Canada's home, believe me." Bobby got out and went around to carry Freda's suitcase to her door. She let herself in.

*

Freda slept through till the the next morning and the first thing she did upon waking was call Cape Breton.

"How are yas making out down there? Long winter?"

"Mom! 'Bout time you called. Are you coming home?"

"Not for a bit yet. Is it mild?"

"Yes, it's been really good since we got the baby home. I bet there hasn't been three feet that fell the whole winter, and here we are now into March."

"Well, love, I got some news."

"What?"

"I'm getting married."

"I see."

"No, I am! He's from out here. His name is Yin."

"Tell us another one."

"It's true. He's Chinese."

"Are you drunk?"

"Gloria, I can't talk to you if you're going to go on like this."

"What do you frigging well expect? I never hear from you! You haven't written once and now you're getting married! You're not even there two months yet."

"Yes, I am. And it's true. We're having a small wedding here, a priest from the Philippines is doing it this coming Tuesday. Wilena's my bridesmaid."

"God Almighty, Chinese, Philippines. What's out there, the United Nations?"

"Pretty near."

"If you're frigging with me, Mom, I'll never forgive you. But if it is true, then you know we're all proud of you here. Just get home soon, and bring him along. What's it, *Jin?*"

"Yin."

"Which makes you Yang, I suppose."

"Something like that. I'll let you go, I would have told you earlier...Listen, don't go spreading it around too much now, will ya. Eyebrows will be leaping right off foreheads when they catch wind of this one."

"Don't worry. I guess it's congratulations, Mom. We love you."

Freda put down the receiver and felt the best she had for days. The call had been on her mind, and now it was over and done. She sat for a time enjoying the feeling when the buzzer for the front entrance sounded. She got up and walked over to the intercom. Pressing the button, she spoke in a deep voice:

"God speaking. Do you want to come up, sinner?"

"I'll sinner ya. And hey, God, find your own joke! Now move your arse and get down here. I got on a light jacket and I'm froze slap to death."

Freda put on her coat, locked things up, and went down to meet her friend. Before leaving for Hong Kong, Freda had been getting together with Wilena for lunch regularly. Most every day they would go down to Denman Street to eat pizza slices in the young English girl's shop. The whole way over Wilena would gripe about the cold. Today was no different.

"The usual, loves, is it?" asked the girl. "Pepperoni for Wilener, salami with whole wheat crust for Freder."

They had her name, too: Victoria. Victoria from England, they called her, or English Victoria. She was trying to save enough money to study geology at UBC.

They carried their big slices to the back of the shop and sat below the TV, which was reporting on the trial.

"Yin asked me last night why they were dragging out this trial so long for. I had no answer for him."

Wilena had pizza in her mouth.

"I got an answer for him, for both of yas," she chewed. "Look, give it enough time and every deed becomes innocent. Simple as that—time. It's the one thing that cleans everything. Of course, thur's only one other thing in the world that keeps a deed dirty, that's conscience. Conscience is on the inside, though, and if a person has no conscience, well then. You and me, and most other people, are what's normal. But not everyone's like that. These lawyers that're doing the defending want us all sick to death of the trial. It's a fact, the arms that hold the pointing fingers will get tired and will want to be put down. It's only natural. The clever bastards know this, it's common sense, mostly. Time. Anyone who defends people deals in it."

"You're all riled up. And where's Bobby, I haven't seen him for a long time. He hasn't been over to play crib. Maybe we should pay him a little visit?"

"Nah, he's all mixed up with this Jorge business. Helping him out with his immigration, trying to keep him in the country. I feel sorry for him—not Bobby, the Mexican fella. He only wants a job, and to settle down someplace, but I guess down at Immigration they got his number. They got wind of him working as a visitor or something like that. Me and you are the only ones who got it all figured out, Freda. Eh?"

"You keep saying. Well, I hope he gets it straightened out. As far as I'm concerned he's a grand fellow."

"Hang on," said Freda, and hollered over to English Victoria. "Excuse me! Victoria? Listen, I want to invite you to a wedding at the church a few streets up from here, on Tuesday. Will you come?"

"Whose is it?"

"Mine."

"You aren't serious!"

"English Victoria, have I ever told you a lie? My generation doesn't fool around, or so Wilena here tells me."

"Good for you! What time is it on then, and where is it again?"

Freda gave her the details, then she sat back to wait for Wilena, who always hoed into her food at the beginning of a meal but slowed for the last few bites.

Before the two parted company for the afternoon, they made plans to get together for cards in the evening. Freda was off to speak to the priest concerning the marriage course she and Tet-Yin were on, a crash marriage course, as the Father had called it. He had designed it especially for them because, supposedly, the two knew what they were doing. The regular course took six months! When Freda learned that, she had said, "Take us quick, or not at all."

*

On Tuesday afternoon the rain was spilling from the heavens. Bobby was driving Freda to the church. Wilena was in the car, and so was Jorge.

"Ju looks good, Freda. In Mexico if it have rain at the wedding day, they say it mean many childrens."

"They say that in Cape Breton, too," said Wilena. "But only the Catholics. But they probably got an expression for hail, fog, snow, or thunder. Any weather is good for them when it comes to you-know-what."

Bobby looked over at Freda and said she looked very smart in her grey pant suit trimmed with a red corsage. Her hair was fixed in a tidy way and her eyeglasses were shiny clean, new looking.

Bobby parked alongside Tet-Yin's car at the church. The men opened the umbrellas for Freda and Wilena to walk under. Inside, a handful of people sat quietly at the very front. Most were Tet-Yin's family. They turned, their faces drawing together to see. Freda and the others were doing the same when a set of hands clamped down on the keys of an organ to produce heavy, extended chords. It was the priest himself playing. The Wedding March!

Wilena stuffed a small bouquet of flowers into Freda's hands and told her to go. The smell of incense filled the church. As she walked up the aisle, Freda thought of the dying man who had come to the church to talk to the priest. She wanted to see him there among the pews. She wanted to tell him first-hand that he was welcome to join in the celebration, from start to finish. He would eagerly participate, too, she imagined. His hair would be wet, but he would be wearing good clothes despite the rain. She would keep track of him during the mass. Solemn and steady, he would look up at them, his uncut hair hanging in strips from a bald top, which would suit him, so it was fine. Charlie would be his name, but Charles he'd prefer. He would listen attentively to all the words, to all the vows, and more so than anyone else in the church, including the priest. Afterwards, at the reception, getting up to say a few words first, he'd finally sing them some old Irish ballad in a beautiful, beautiful voice…

Tet-Yin's face came sharply into focus. Freda took his hand. It was thick and very clean, and it felt cool and warm. She figured that his blood circulation must not be all that good, or that he was nervous. He was freshly washed. Nice. She looked at him, she breathed in his smell. They straightened for the priest. His priestly gowns were slightly too big for him, but his round chest and shoulders held them up well enough.

Trying to take his time, but having no stories for them today, the priest went through the ceremony quickly. Tet-Yin put the ring on Freda's finger. She watched her new son-in-law, who had passed over the ring. She smiled at him but did not have even the slightest recollection of what his name was. It'll come later, she thought. Then there was Mei-Mei, the bingo star. Silent now, beautiful now, she had the role of flower girl. The others were in the pews. In her throat, Freda felt a kindness for every single one. She was trying to turn back to look at her own party when Tet-Yin began the kiss. Not having a chance to close her eyes, she saw Bobby, Jorge and Wilena looking at her. With them was English Victoria, in a smart green skirt and blue sweater, her face a perfect painting with tears streamig down. Then the kiss was over; they were man and wife. The assembly applauded. Freda threw the bouquet out into the aisle. Pei-Jung caught it and held it against her neck.

"You have to marry a Canadian boy now!" Wilena called out from the side.

"No! Canadian boy have too long hair!"

Even the priest laughed. After the signing of the documents, the party left the church and, taking out their umbrellas, hurried to the cars. Puddles were everywhere in the parking lot. The plan was to gather at the same restaurant they had visited the night after bingo.

When everyone had arrived and was seated, Jorge stood up.

"Sit down!" said Bobby.

"No! Ju sit down if ju want! I am not afraid, this is a wedding....Now Freda, ju and Yin is married and I wish for jour happiness. I am very proud." But he could not go on. He stood for a long moment unable to move. No one said anything. Then fat tears started rolling down his face, too many for him to brush away.

"Sit down, you clown!" said Bobby. "Do you want to ruin it?" That broke the spell, and Jorge smiled, then obediently took his seat.

Wilena followed suit. She was on her feet and looked very short in the formal clothes she was wearing. Her gloves nearly reached her elbows. Balancing herself and blinking back the tiny tears collected at the sides of her eyes, she paused.

"Freda, Yin...I care for you both, a whole lot. You show and give the rest of us courage. Yous'll always be in my thoughts." There was clapping, and she sat. The waiter they had hired wanted to bring the set lunch but Pei-Jung, feeling the need, got up next.

"Grandfather, Freda. We wish you a happy life together and a healthy baby boy."

She sat and everyone looked around. Tet-Yin explained that this was the translation of a standard Chinese blessing wished for newly married couples. They ate heartily.

The next day the new couple found an apartment between Wilena's place and Tet-Yin's daughter's. Having talked it over, they both agreed that community was most important. An apartment would free up Tet-Yin; his house had been a great burden, and he put it on the market. The new place was on Cardero Street, which crossed Davie. On one of the lawns nearby was a ten-foot wooden sunflower, which Freda thought would make a good landmark to remind them they were home.

April came, but the skies took no real notice. It remained wet, sombre. But the month was a good one to have the house for sale; there had been two offers and a lot of inquiries. The real estate agent said it would go before summer. The newlyweds were ready for their honeymoon.

"Ingonish! Where else?" Freda told Bobby and Wilena. She and Tet-Yin were playing partners against them at Wilena's. Tet-Yin knew the rules by heart now despite still being slow at counting up his hands.

"This game give me two things," he told them.

"And what are they?" asked Wilena.

"Stress and pressure."

"Make one more mistake and I'll include a third thing," said Freda. "A braining."

"But won't thur be six feet of snow in Ingonish?" said Wilena.

"Go on with ya! And if that's the case, that's fine. I'll take snow over this rain any day. It gets you down, because it never lets up."

"In Hong Kong it rains more worse," said Tet-Yin, laying down a cool hand of sixteen points.

"Yin's going to run away with the pig!" said Bobby. "So to speak, I mean…They say that in California."

Freda looked at him. "Do they?…Anyway, it'll be warm enough soon. We're going to spend up till the end of June there. I've got to take care of the old place, you know—storm windows, hooking up the power, water, the like. I could be selling it yet, I don't know. I expect the family will run me out of town completely if I do. Give us a spot more tea, Wilena."

"Get your own," said Wilena, not looking up from her cards. Freda poured tea for everyone.

"Why don't you and Bobby take a trip home yourselves?" she said. "It's all you ever talk about."

"Good idea," said Tet-Yin. "Every night we can play cribs there."

"Yes now," said Wilena. "As if I got nothing better to do. And the money, where's that supposed to come from, a tree out back?"

"You!" said Freda. "Go bag your head, you got more money than I don't know who. Tell her Bobby."

"You decide to Mom, and I'll see if I can't get my vacation around then."

"Yas're all ganging up on me! Let's us just get back to the game at hand here and not have anymore talk about anything else."

Chapter 12

Husband and wife arrived at the Sydney Airport, and were met by Gloria and Jimmy. Freda gave them both a hug and took the baby.

"Little Freda," she said. "This is your new granddaddy, Yin!"

Tet-Yin hugged Gloria and shook Jimmy's hand.

"Where's Bradley?" said Freda. "Too busy shooting birds to come and see his dear old grandmother?"

"He's in school today."

They went outside toward the car. The parking lot had icy patches, and Jimmy was holding Gloria by the shoulders. Tet-Yin stopped to look up at the sky. He said the area was beautiful. When everyone was in the car, Jimmy lit a cigarette and pulled away hard, sending the car spinning left then right over the ice. He hauled up on the emergency brake and the car did a doughnut.

"Yee haw!" He looked devilishly back at Freda.

"Smarten the frig up, Jimmy!" Gloria said. "Don't be such a clown—and put that smoke out! Nice way to introduce Jin to where we live."

"*Yin!*" said Freda. "And don't let me have to repeat it again."

She turned to Tet-Yin, "See what I had to live with? No wonder I left."

Jimmy began to talk to the newcomer, and Freda caught up on the news with Gloria. It felt good to know Tet-Yin was being made welcome. Kelly's Mountain, the big emptiness of St. Anne's Bay, and the end-of-the-world feel of the north shore greeted them. Tet-Yin shifted his weight back and forth to see as much as he could. Freda tried to imagine what it must be like to see it all for the first time. It must look Scottish, she thought, but then what did that look like? At least there must be a simple, country feel to it. The excitement registered on Tet-Yin's face in his eagerness to pay attention to the Jimmy's narration.

"Yes, Jin," Jimmy said. "God's country here, me son."

"Very beautiful," he said. "More different than Vancouver."

Freda looked out, too, and was glad to be home, glad to have cheated another winter, and this one properly.

When they reached the base of Cape Smokey, she started a decade of the beads, with Gloria saying the refrain. Jimmy had both hands on the wheel and his head against the glass of his window. Tet-Yin, still wide-eyed, still pitching himself forward at the scenes, at last saw where the ocean waves were snapping at the ice along the shore. Freda slapped his shoulder and told him to be still, that his weight was throwing the car around, and they would go down over the bank if he didn't smarten up.

Near the top of the mountain, the car took the twists slowly. It swayed right of centre then close to the shoulder while the final Hail Marys and Our Fathers were said. At the crest of the mountain, the women stopped praying. Jimmy pulled off to the side and got out.

"I think I got a flat." He shut the door and in a moment stuck his head back in. "Freda, get out here and change this." Grinning, he reached for his pack of cigarettes. Gloria told him to shut the door because the baby was getting cold.

"Is the tire flat?" asked Tet-Yin.

"No, he always gets out here. He'll be right back."

Tet-Yin got out of the car and inspected the tires. They were low but fine. Jimmy stood between the car and the guardrail, looking down at the sea. He told Tet-Yin that the ice comes from far up north and a northeast wind was bringing it ashore today. He pointed to where, in a day, it had swept almost the entire length of the north shore, where they had just come down. It moves every day, he said. The sun in the afternoon sky lit the planes and pitches of jumbled ice to a silver; parts the sun could not reach were white or shadowed.

"An arctic wind always comes in off it. See those black things? Watch them, they're moving."

Tet-Yin said nothing.

"Those are seals," said Jimmy. "You know, ohh-ohhh!" He imitated the animal, and Tet-Yin smiled.

"Ah, delicious?"

"What! Delicious? Me son—get in the car. The wind's coming under the skin and entering the bones. The best is yet to come." He started back for the door.

"Yin fixed her," he said to the others and let Tet-Yin get in the back first. Jimmy got in and twisted his cigarette out in the ashtray. Gloria told him to keep it away from the baby. They drove on and now there was plenty of braking and shifting. Jimmy made an announcement when they had dropped one thousand feet. "This is the start to Ingonish," he said to Tet-Yin, pointing to a small green sign that read Ingonish Ferry. The car coasted and wound to an opening where they could see the harbour.

"Something else, wha?" said Jimmy.

The harbour seemed to be gushing out to welcome their loaded car as it came down off the steeps of Ingonish Ferry. A solid, still layer of ice lay below a higher, heavy-looking layer of water. Jimmy rolled down his window.

"Jimmy, you'll freeze us all! Have a little sense, will ya." Gloria tucked the blanket in around the baby's face.

"Keep you're drawers on, dear. I'm only airing the car out a bit, giving Yin and Freda a lungful of what true fresh air is." The car then drove its way down around the turns below the ski hill, and everyone saw that the ski lift was operating. At the top, there were exposed patches of dirt. Bright flicks and flashes came from skis or poles where skiers crossed in the sun.

"Did yas eat yet?" said Gloria. "I got some stew left over from yesterday. We'll have that when we get home." She looked out the window. "This year the winter is nice, but I find it the worst when the seasons change."

The car was now at the head of the harbour and Freda was staring out the window on her side. Here, she always felt the journey was over. She turned and looked up the valley, then even higher up, where the barrens began. It was still very frosty looking there.

"Look at boys!" said Tet-Yin.

Kids were playing on broken ice near the shore, navigating sections of it in the open water, using long poles.

"Don't mind them fools," said Jimmy. "We call that activity 'jumping clampours.' A good way to get your death." Everyone in the car looked down as the boys pushed small and large trapeziums of ice along the shore. It was slow, heavy work. Askew on each head was a woolen stocking hat, and at least one boy had on worksocks for mittens. Their faces were smiling and red, their expressions youthful and saucy. Jimmy rolled down the window.

"Yas wanna be kilt! Get home you little pack of fools!" One boy dropped his pole and with both hands grabbed his crotch.

"See what that little bastard did to me! I should stop the car."

"They'd get a murdering all right if they were my kids," said Freda.

"Once," said Jimmy, "we were out so far on the ice off the Centre that the old man and the old lady could see us from the kitchen window. They were inside having a cup of tea. You imagine, that far out. Did we ever get some good old-fashioned arse tanning when we got home."

Freda looked over at Tet-Yin and brushed at the fur of his leather jacket. He was looking contemplatively out the window and his face was smooth. He looked to be concentrating on where he was. God love him, Freda thought. He doesn't understand all this but he is trying. This trip will be good for him, he has the right idea on how to handle it already. Freda adjusted herself in her seat, then told Tet-Yin that the flat area they were passing was the spot for good fresh clams in the summer. The road straightened and sank. Jimmy slowed so Tet-Yin could get a good look out over the side.

"Yes, Jin, out there," Jimmy said. "All the clams you would ever want, and you don't have to pay a red cent."

"Really, you don't have pay?" He looked down at the ice-covered area. Dark silt had risen from faults in the ice. Jimmy pressed in the cigarette lighter, and when it snapped back out, lit another cigarette. "Just having a drag or two," he said into the rear-view mirror, where he could see Freda glaring at him.

"Get your window down a bit then." Freda kept her gaze on the way Jimmy held the cigarette between his fingers as he drove, how he squinted when he held it to his mouth. He looked smart smoking. It was as if he was figuring things out, thought Freda. He likely was. When he first started coming around to see Gloria, that was the thing she criticized him about, his smoking. Now that she knew him, it was something she didn't mind, except for the effect on the baby of course.

*

Jimmy put the cigarette in his mouth when steering the wheel to get the car into the yard. He eased in on the brakes but could not stop the tires from locking. The car slipped through the icy tire grooves near the house before gently pushing in against a snowbank, dirty and hard, near the porch.

"Made her," he said and switched off the engine. They got out, and Freda's first thought was how utterly quiet it all was.

Gloria was holding the baby again. "She's a lovely child," said Freda. "Not a peep out of her the whole way down. She must take after me." At the entrance, Jimmy had thrown down plenty of gravel already but now added more. The sidewalk was icy and hard in the shadows of the gables.

"Quiet?" said Gloria. "Hope you'll say that tonight when she's screaming blue murder and won't go to sleep. You'll see who she takes after then."

They went into the house and Freda welcomed Tet-Yin. The others welcomed him. Freda walked into the kitchen, which now seemed smaller and darker. The smell of drying birch sticks was all through the house. The wood was behind the stove.

"Angus!" Jimmy hollered. "Get out here and meet your new brother-in-law!"

From the living room, where the TV was going quietly, came a lanky straight figure with a nose wide like a bottle opener. His eyes were icy blue, his skin healthy.

"Oh, how are ya, dear," he said, going over to Freda. He shook Tet-Yin's hand and said hello. "Did yas have a good trip?"

"Yes, clear sailing. Not a drop of traffic on the roads."

"I seen the salt truck go up a while ago," he said. "I thought there might be some frost on Smokey. It snowed earlier."

Jimmy filled the kettle from the tap. "No, it was a good trip. Thought I had a flat when we got up over the mountain, but when Jin and me got out to assess the situation we discovered that it was just the weight of Freda sitting over the wheel well."

Gloria put the baby to bed and came back into the kitchen to serve stew from the pot that had been simmering on the stove. Freda and Tet-Yin were seated at the table. Jimmy offered Tet-Yin a pair of wool work socks; Freda told him to take them. Angus made the tea.

"All right, Freda, what the frig you been up to?" he said.

"Not much."

"Not much! Yes, now. Tell us about your travels! And what in the old dying is this about you getting married?"

"Not much to say, Angy. I went out to see my friend Wilena then got used to living out there. I met some good people, then Yin and

I here started frigging around with each other. You can imagine the rest."

"Mom!" said Gloria, who was tapping Angus on the elbow to let her get at the stew.

"Ya haven't changed, Freda," said Angus. "Still with the sharp tongue. You always had that." He went for a dry piece of wood in the other room.

"Don't you start, Eddy Angus! Or I'll put you in your place," called Freda after him. Jimmy was looking at Tet-Yin, grinning and winking. Steam rose from their bowls of stew, which had a wood-smoke smell to it.

"This is a boiled dinner," Jimmy explained as they all sampled it. "Ya better eat it, too, Jin, or else the chef here'll fly right off the handle and toss you out in the snowbank. She's been known to do it."

Everyone was hungry and only Angus did not have a second bowl.

"This delicious," said Tet-Yin and when offered more, took it.

"Must have been something when you were over there, Freda," Angus said. "Lots of people, eh?"

"Standing room only."

"Holy jumpin'!"

"It'd be like the legion on Saturday night and they were giving away free beer."

"Yesss!" said Angus and Jimmy at the same time. They looked at each other. The dog was at the door. Jimmy rose. The tags on the creature's leash jangled as it came in.

"H.D.! Come here, how's she going fella?" Freda patted the dog, and scratched behind its ears. It went over to its empty dish, sniffed, then came back to her.

"What's name?" Tet-Yin asked.

"H.D.," said Jimmy. "That's short for hound dog. No one would name him when we got him, so I think it was you, Freda, who started it. She called him what he was, and it stuck." The dog was wagging his tail now in recognition and Freda kept petting him.

"To tell the truth, he's just an old black mongrel that come around here to eat one day and stayed. He's probably got more fathers than what's in the Catholic Church." The dog went over and buried his snout in Tet-Yin's crotch, which made Tet-Yin laugh. He gently pushed the animal away.

"H.D., go lay down! Where's this little grandson of mine?" said Freda. "Some manners now. I come all the way back, and he isn't here to greet me."

"He'll be up soon," said Gloria. "He's likely down the rock or the shore with the Donovan kids. I'll go screech for him." She went outside, and did just that.

"Jimmy," said Angus, his arms crossed high now and shoulders raised because of the heat from the stove. "Why don't ya give the man here an old haul on that fiddle of yours. I'm sure Freda could do with hearing a tune, too, after being away so long. What do you say, Jin?" said Angus looking at the guest and making the odd gesture of a fiddle playing.

"*Yin*, Angus. All of yas, his name is Yin," said Freda. "And don't let me have to say it again."

"That's what I said," said Angus.

"Yes," said Tet-Yin to Angus. "You play?"

"Now, Angus, what did you bring that up for?" said Jimmy. "You know I can't play the frigging thing, especially for people. You always do that. Besides, my bridge is gone."

"What happened to the bridge?"

"She got washed out in a rainstorm last fall," said Jimmy, and Angus spilled the tea he was drinking. He put down the cup to laugh better.

"What are you laughing at, you old hawk?" Freda threw a pair of work socks at Angus. "Give us one then, Jimmy."

"Go on, Freda. It sounds like a cat fight when I get playing," said Jimmy, standing to undo the clasps of his fiddle case. He lifted the instrument and plucked the four strings, then went back to the stove and sat. Positioning it on his shoulder, he angled it so that he could get at the strings with the bow. He liked to play between the window and the stove; he liked to occupy all the space there. Without giving thought to rosin, the bow, or to checking the tuning, he started up with a coarse piece, something that immediately livened up the whole house. Freda didn't know the name of this piece, but it was a hard one, and she was impressed by how good it sounded.

Angus put his tea in a safe place and pulled away from the heat of the stove. He bent near the door to pull on a pair of insulated workboots then straight away began dancing. He came down on the kitchen oilcloth with his boots, laces flicking, and made an awful racket.

"Come, Freda, on your feet! You know this!" He raised her by the fingertips and she began by clapping along then dropped her hands to step the tune out in her feet. The dog came between them to chase his tail around, and leapt up against the dancers' thighs. The floor joists dipped under the pounding of Angus' boots. Tet-Yin's neck was raised so that his fat there was taut. With his eyes wide, he was smiling and laughing and clapped along.

When Jimmy launched into "Old King's Reel," Angus looked as if he were at the beginnings of a fit. He appeared to be trying his best to take apart the floorboards with his feet, his knees bending like the corners of a cardboard box. Gloria came in the door with Bradley. The boy smiled first then jumped to the floor. Freda took him by the hands.

Gloria laughed, then shouted seriously, "Angus! Take it easy on the frigging floor with those big boots!" Jimmy had his eyes closed and the fiddle on his shoulder looked to have lightened to the weight of an alder switch. Suddenly the jabbing of his bow got tangled up in the curtains, and he was forced to finish the set with the curtains and rods coming tumbling down on top of him. Everyone applauded, and Gloria walked over to slap him in the head. He smiled modestly out from under the heap. Angus knit his fingers over his stomach and let out a hoot, then hugged Freda.

"Ah, sister," he said.

"Great!" said Tet-Yin. "Great, great! Did you take lesson?" Tet-Yin was still clapping. Jimmy got himself untangled and was setting the curtain rod and curtains back in place. He loosened the tension of his bow then sat again, the fiddle upright on his thigh.

"When I was a young fella I did, Jin. But just one. When I turned twenty, I said to myself, 'That's it, I'm gonna play the fiddle. That's what I'll do.' The old man could play, and they always said that music was in the blood, so this one day after going up to North Sydney and buying the whole package—fiddle, rosin, bow, and case—and damn near spending my whole paycheque, I came down to the house with case and all. I went out to the back where Dad was working. He saw me coming. It was a sunny day and he was shingling a new piece of the house. I guess a new baby had been born or something. 'Father,' I sang out. 'See what I got here. I'm all set to play, so give us a lesson!' He was busy, but I remember feeling in my heart that this was what he had probably said to his old man when he was young.

"So he looks and squints at me. In his mouth, a couple three-quarter-inch nails; a shingle in one hand, his hammer in the other. He says, 'Open 'er up,' so I undo the case over my knee. 'See that long thing inside,' he says. 'That's a bow. You take that and scratch it back and forth across the strings till a tune comes out.' He turns back to his shingling as if I was never there. That was my lesson, Jin." Jimmy had his cup of tea and drank from it.

"What in the old dying frig was he doing shingling the house with three-quarter-inch nails?" asked Angus.

"Don't know, me son. That's all he had to work with in those days, I suppose. Those old fellas liked their nails bigger anyway. Many of the houses around here probably got the bigger nails in them, which might be why you never see them being repaired. The older ones are way stronger than the newer ones."

Gloria said she was going to lie down. Freda and Tet-Yin went for a rest, too. Angus went back in to the TV, and Jimmy and Bradley left in the car to get some groceries.

After a short lie-down, Freda and Tet-Yin went outside. There was plenty of sun left in the Ingonish sky. It still had to drop a good bit to reach the heavy mountains rising in behind the woods. The whole bay below was jammed to the shore with ice. Freda pointed out the bill of Smokey and asked Tet-Yin if he remembered driving over it. The rocks looked sore pink in the sun and broke the blueness of the sky in behind and all the way down to the ice.

"This is not same country for me," said Tet-Yin. "It is too difficult to understand people here."

"Are you having trouble? Give it a little while."

She led him up to a higher plane, above Jimmy and Gloria's house. They could see Jimmy; he was outside putting windshield-washer fluid in his car. The hood was up, and music drifted out an open door.

"This is my house here," said Freda when they had reached an old house at the top of the hill. All the windows on the first floor were covered with sheets of plywood. Jimmy had been good enough to secure the place before Freda left, and he had told her on the phone that he was keeping an eye on it.

The front door came open with a yank. The whole front of the house, which had been built facing south, was cold in shadow. Tet-Yin had to help Freda get the inside door open, which was swollen with moisture. It was cold and black inside, and the air had an unhealthy feel to it.

"The electricity and water are shut off," said Freda. "I drained the pipes myself before I left because I didn't know how long I was going to be away."

Tet-Yin walked into the kitchen, his footwear loud over the floor.

"You live here?" He went to the wood stove and looked toward the bare kitchen table. "Is here where you play cribs?"

"The odd game."

Freda moved inside the kitchen also and gazed at the stove. The grates looked thick and cold. To prevent rusting, she had put a layer of lard over it. Stepping closer now, she saw a fine dust covered the greased surface.

"This will all burn off when I light it," she said. "At least I hope it will. I never done it before. Let's go, Tets. This house is too cold, too full of memories."

She spoke the truth, especially about the memories—the place was teeming, but she was resisting them. Later perhaps, she told herself; not now, not in the cold, dark quiet of a finished winter. Putting her hand on Tet-Yin's shoulder, she led them back outside and pulled the door shut.

The next evening, Freda stole from the house with a flashlight and moved up the hill toward her own house. Once inside, she wandered from room to room, going first into the living room, then into the parlour. Stopping in the back bedroom, she threw the light on the bed a moment, but then left quickly. In the kitchen, she pointed the flashlight down at the floor and looked out the window at the dark. Picking up the light again, she shone it in through the dining room along the tiles, some of which were cracked at the corners and warped. Milton put these tiles down, she recalled as she moved forward into the room. It was just after their new son was brought home from the hospital and she had him placed close to the stove in a cradle. Freda went to the cellar for a scuttle of coal, and as she was coming back up, she paused to look in at her young husband. Beyond was the window where the sun was entering but a cold wind was at the back corner of the house, making the dining room drafty. The day was not fit to be outside.

Milton wore his shirt open at the throat, his hair oiled, and his sideburns trimmed. She could smell the glue he was using and see it stuck to his knees and where the loose tiles were sticking to his pants. Owning a house and doing its upkeep were new to him then, and naturally he never liked to show his inexperience. Freda was sure he knew she was there watching. He gave her his profile, kept poised and contemplative while his wife looked in at him, her husband. The oil stove hummed and Freda heard the baby kick, but she stood still. She couldn't move she had been so happy. And now she couldn't move because she was so sad.

There was someone at the door.

"Mom? You up here?" It was Gloria. "What's wrong?" Gloria stood out by the entrance and would not advance down the hallway.

"What are you doing up here in the dark?"

She came closer and Freda, looking away, raised her arm to her eyes.

"Just looking is all," she answered, but in a low voice as if speaking to herself.

"Well come back up here in the kitchen."

The two went in and stood by the table. Gloria reached up and lowered an oil lantern from the shelf and got her mother to shine the light on the matches she took from the top of the stove. She lit the lantern and the two women sat. Gloria looked across at her mother.

"I'll help you clean this," she said, searching her mother's eyes. The lantern created waving shadows of their sitting figures on the walls, shadows that flared when the oil on the wick sputtered.

"He's a nice fellow; Jimmy won't shut up about him."

"He is good, Gloria. Of course, you know he's not our kind, whatever that's supposed to mean. I couldn't, Gloria, with all respect to your father. I know I probably have the strength in me, but if you find someone to make them long hours go easier..."

"There's no need to explain. I know, Mom. I just want to say you were not in good shape when you left. But you went. Few would, but you did. And you should see the change in yourself. As far as I'm concerned, it's the greatest thing in the world."

Freda looked at her daughter's brown wavy hair, at her eyes and at her face, but could only see herself. Her youth, her spark, all the playfulness—it was all there. And listen to her here, thought Freda, opening up to her mother. Something I don't know if I ever did, or ever could have done.

"You're your father through and through," said Freda. "I never told you but he was the shiest man in Ingonish when I first met him, and he never had a bad word to say about anyone. That's you, Gloria."

"I'm also you, don't forget."

"Oh, I don't forget that."

"I'll give you a hand with the cleaning in here. Of course, you could always stay at the house, but I know how you are. We'll give it a go in the morning, first thing. We'll get the heat on and open the windows, let the fellas tackle the outside."

Freda looked down at her daughter's hand, which she was now holding. The light from the lantern was making shadows at the knuckles. Freda turned to the window; three reflections of the lantern were in the glass.

"It's just coming back here, Gloria. I see that now. It's this house and things I thought I'd dealt with."

"Well, there might always be things you have to deal with, there always are with anyone. And I know that sounds easy when someone else says it. You got someone here, though, someone to make it a good place with, someone like you, who's not afraid. Let's go back down to the house. I should check on the baby."

Gloria picked up the flashlight from the table, and after waiting for her mother, blew out the lantern through the top of the glass shade. The two left the kitchen, the floor giving off an aching sound as they passed over it in the dark.

CHAPTER 13

The following weeks saw the arrival of the season with scents and burgeoning life, the scars of snow quickly fading. Freda and Tet-Yin were living in her house on the hill. The electricity was hooked up and all the storm windows had been taken off. Freda said she was going to put a coat of paint on the old place when it warmed up a little more.

Tet-Yin was comfortable enough with life in Ingonish. He was quiet during the day, but it was a peaceful silence. Despite her worries that he would not take to the place, Freda saw that he was able to occupy himself. All in all, he was a patient man.

Together, he and Freda had put a garden in when the risk of frost was gone. Beans were sprouting up over the tilled soil now, and Tet-Yin checked on their progress first thing every morning. He always had reports for Freda at breakfast. They had also put in carrots, parsnips, and turnips. These plants were starting to push through the soil as well. The smell of growing lupines entered the house as soon as the weather was fine enough to leave the front door open. Freda had planted the wildflowers years ago, and now they took complete charge of the front yard.

On many evenings, Tet-Yin spent time with Jimmy. They would go up the Clyburn River to fly-fish. Tet-Yin had always wanted to try it. Jimmy had taken him to Sydney and they bought all the gear. A little nervous at the beginning, he got the hang of it soon enough. He now carried a little vial of handmade flies with him everywhere and would often take them out and admire his collection.

One night, he and Jimmy brought home a salmon. Freda thought she had lost him over to Jimmy completely when she found the two sitting on lawn chairs on Jimmy's new verandah, smoking.

"You don't smoke!" But she had seen him smoke once, during Chinese New Year in Hong Kong, at a family gathering in his daughter's home. That was Chinese New Year, though.

"He caught a fish," said Jimmy, the pair of them sitting like bad little boys. Tet-Yin laughed from his lawn chair and dangled his legs outwards.

"You did?"

"He did! Me and him were at the hole below the swinging bridge for a little bit, just checking on if there was any action there. Then we came down by number six and weren't there fifteen minutes when he had himself a bite and hauls this in. He's a fisherman, Freda. I got a bite too, but he got away."

Freda asked for a cigarette, and Tet-Yin watched her take it.

"Don't everyone start smoking now," said Jimmy said. "Yas'll have me in the poorhouse!" Freda sat on the arm of Tet-Yin's chair. Jimmy rose and went in the house, and came back with his fiddle. He started off with some slow tunes at low volume. He shut his eyes.

Freda got up after smoking half the cigarette and tossed it over the side of the verandah. She went inside and, after a spell, returned with some tea. She set down the cups, canned milk, and sugar on the empty cable spool they used for a table. She pulled a chair over, and she and Tet-Yin started to drink as Jimmy finished his tune.

Cars passed on the road. Jimmy and Gloria's house was situated near a sharp turn. Lots of cars were on the road tonight. The nice weather brought them. When rounding the turn, passengers and drivers alike would be focused and looking serious. Out of the sharp turn though, they always looked in at Jimmy's place, especially at the new verandah; and if Jimmy was outside with the violin, their faces would fall apart in smiles and horns would toot.

Freda told Tet-Yin to wave back when the cars passed, and he was happy to oblige. Some cars even had their windows partway down. It isn't that warm out, thought Freda. God love them though, windows down, reaching out for the idea of summer and who cares if they're freezing themselves in the process?

"Here he comes," said Jimmy, the fiddle end resting on his knee, "Walking Jim Antichrist." A car pulled in the yard. It was Hector and Harold, Jimmy's brothers. Hector was the quiet one. He didn't drink. Harold, on the other hand, was a different story. They got out of the car.

"G'day, boys," said Jimmy.

"G'day," said Hector taking a seat at the end of the verandah.

"Some evening," said Harold. "No flies." He bent one leg up on the step. Freda introduced the men to Tet-Yin, and they waved. Harold leaned into the railing. He was the tallest of the three brothers. They all had the same black eyes and black bushy eyebrows.

"I just seen that old Joe Jeezer that called the cops on us last Saturday," said Harold.

"Who?" asked Jimmy.

"That slimy next-door neighbour of mine. Oh, dying Jesus, how I'd like to get a slap at him!" Harold was always rowing with his neighbour over something. This particular incident started when the neighbour accused Harold of building a shed on his property. They used to drink together, but now it was a run at who would be first to drive the other out.

"Why can't you let sleeping dogs lie?" said Jimmy. "What's the use in starting a war? You were in the wrong with the shed, the man has his rights. Learn to take things a little easier like Hector over there."

"Oh, thur won't be a war. Not after I give him his teeth to drink."

At the end of the verandah Hector laughed down into the dirt. Harold went inside to talk to Gloria and when he returned he had a cup of water in his hand. Hector would not accept anything when he went to someone's home.

Harold resumed his position against the railing after setting his cup down on it. He lit a smoke, breathed some of it in, then exhaled audibly. With the cigarette between his fingers, he scratched roughly and quickly at his scalp, a little ash falling off there. He told Tet-Yin that a good friend of his from trade school had worked for a time on the oil rigs off Singapore and Indonesia, and said he liked it over there, too.

"Isn't his son going somewhere like that in the fall?" asked Jimmy. "That's right, yeah, he's heading out in the fall. Going to Japan teaching," said Harold. "Thur all doing that now."

"What city?"

"Seoul."

"Go home, fool," said Jimmy. "Seoul ain't in Japan!"

"Where is it then, Ranald?"

"India."

"Wha? India, go home!" said Harold. "And how in the old dying frig are you supposed to know where it's at anyway? Someone who's never even been over the Causeway before."

"Yeah, well, at least I ain't afraid ta leave the house."

"Simmer down, the two of yas," said Freda. "We got someone right here to settle the score. Ask him where this place is yas're getting all hot and bothered over."

Tet-Yin told them where Seoul was. Hector watched when Tet-Yin spoke, nodding his head and listening carefully. Tet-Yin had been there, and he said that the people there ate dogs. He mentioned this detail only because he was learning from Jimmy how to keep the conversation going strong.

"Suppose!" said Hector from his place on the step.

"That right?" said Harold, slapping at a blackfly on the fat part of his arm.

"The white dog taste more better than the black one," said Tet-Yin.

"Me son!" said Jimmy. "Bring them over here, they'll have some fine pickings in Ingonish."

"Jimmy!" said Freda. "Nice mouth. A woman's present you know, and here yas're are talking about eating dogs."

"Did I say it? Did I bring it up?"

"No, but you provoked it. You think I don't know what effect you're having?"

It was getting dark, and the flies were bad now. Jimmy started up his fiddle but didn't finish the tune. The flies were eating him alive, so he lit a smoke to keep them away. Tet-Yin stayed on the verandah after Harold and Hector left in their car, and Freda cleared the tea things away leaving them to talk about fishing.

*

On a Saturday morning in late August, a strange looking van pulled up the drive to Freda's house. She was out back in the garden with Tet-Yin, and they were on their knees weeding. Tet-Yin pushed a bowl of tomatoes ahead of him as he pulled weeds. It had been a good summer for growing. The tomatoes were big, and there were half a dozen jars of rhubarb jam on the kitchen table, which they had prepared the evening before.

Freda walked around to the front of her house to see who it was. Wilena was leaning out the passenger window.

"Look at this," said Freda. "What are you doing here? You didn't even tell me you were coming!"

A door shut and Bobby walked around the front fender, wearing sandals and summer clothes. The side door opened next and out came Jorge, mannerly and smiling; he opened Wilena's door and took her hand. Freda walked over. Jorge's hair was too long, and she touched it.

"My brother Angus has clippers," she said. "We'll get you fixed up later."

She waved her arm to start them all for the house, but they wanted to go out back and have a look at the garden when they learned Tet-Yin was there. He was still on his hands and knees at a row of potatoes, his face beet red. He got himself up and on his feet, then started for them, happy the whole way. With a gloved hand he carried his bowl of tomatoes against his waist. He began to rush, but Freda told him to watch out for the carrots.

"Great! Time to play cribs! Get the board out, Freda, and tea, get the kettle on."

"Don't bark orders out like that at me. I know you're excited."

"Yes, I am!"

They went into the kitchen, where it was cool in the pleasant dimness of a summer morning.

"I suppose you think I was joking about the haircut," Freda said to Jorge. "You need it and you'll get it."

"Jes, is a good idea, no?" said Jorge.

"I wish I needed one," said Bobby sliding his hand over his black bristly hair. "The only thing growing here is my forehead."

"How long yas down for?" asked Freda from the pantry, where water was running. "A little while I hope."

"We're just popping in for a little visit on our way around the Cabot Trail," said Wilena, who was rearranging the jars of rhubarb jam on the table. She turned their labels to face out and then pushed them back in out of the sun. The glass was cool, but their lids were warm where the sun had been coming in through the window.

"She's never ever been around the Trail, Freda," said Bobby. "Can you imagine that? And it always right here in her own backyard. Your own country is the last to get seen, I guess. We are trying to take in all the sights we can before heading back to Vancouver next week."

Freda persuaded them to stay at least the night. Tet-Yin took Bobby and Jorge down to meet Jimmy, but he had already left for work. When they returned Bradley was with them. Everyone climbed in the van and, with Freda's direction, went on a tour of Ingonish. Realizing that there was a lot to see, she had trouble deciding where to go.

They followed a dusty road a long way to a waterfall. When they arrived and had the van parked, Bobby pointed out that all the other cars had Parks Canada vehicle passes on their windshields.

"A quick peek won't hurt," said Freda. The air was fresh and spruce and pine needles lined the wooden walkway leading down to the falls. The water echoed in the trees sheltering the path. They stopped when they could see the falls. In late summer, when the water was less forceful, it spilled beer-coloured into pools. They could see some young fellows at the higher pool, lying on the big, flat rock ledges that went around the outside. They looked to be hard at work enjoying the final days of any real warmth. They wore cut-off jeans and had their hair slicked back. One with a tattoo had a shampoo bottle in one hand and a hairbrush in the other.

"Lots more to see, so let's go," said Freda.

Next they drove to Warren's Lake. Freda said that when she was young, her parents used to take her here for picnics after her father had bought his first car. The lake was very deep, she said. It had been scooped out by the glaciers. Bradley ran down to the edge and started firing rocks at schooling shadows near the shore. There was a wood fire somewhere, in the far corner of the beach where the sand was coarse and stony and the trees came down to the water.

"Look," said Wilena. "A French family, naked."

"How do you know they're French?" said Freda, squinting along with the rest.

"You can hear them, listen…And who else would flap their genitals around in public for all the world to see?" Wilena had her hand flat over the top of her eyeglasses.

"I would," said Bobby.

"Gentles?" said Tet-Yin.

"Bradley!" Freda called out. "Get up here before this gang drives a person batty!"

"We going home now?" Bradley asked as he came closer.

"No, dear. Come on."

From Warren's Lake, they took a quick ride over to the beaches of the Centre and South Bay. The first was not busy at all, but at the second there was not even a place to park. Someone caught a glimpse of golfers on a fairway. This was the road to the Keltic Lodge, explained Freda, the hotel built out on the rocks of Middle Head Peninsula. She asked Bradley if he knew who worked here, but before he could answer they saw Jimmy on the grounds. He was operating a lawn mower, wearing earplugs, and ignoring the van, which was unfamiliar to him.

Freda told Bobby to pull over as close as he could and had all the others, except Wilena, duck down in the back. She instructed Bobby to ask for directions to the Keltic. Bobby waved to Jimmy, who came over, allowing his machine to idle in the shade. He walked up with his earplugs in his hand.

"Sorry to bother you," said Bobby. "Where's the Keltic?"

"You're at it."

"At it?"

"See those big doors over there, this building here with the bright red trim? Well, this is it." Freda, Bradley, Jorge, and Tet-Yin bounced up from the back.

"Freda! Oh dying Jesus—a man's working here!" said Jimmy. "You never stop."

Jimmy introduced himself to Bobby, Wilena, and Jorge. He offered his cigarettes first before lighting one.

"Big party at the house tonight," said Freda. "Bring your fiddle, bring Gloria, and whoever else. See if you can't get Angus up out of his chair, too. And tell him to bring his clippers along."

*

Tet-Yin and Jorge began cooking the lobsters they'd picked up, and both talked a lot during the process. Bobby took a beer and watched them. Freda and Wilena worked together on a big pot of seafood chowder. They put a lot of potatoes in it and used the tomatoes in a salad. Bradley had to go down to his house to get ready for mass, which was at five-thirty.

Freda had Jorge and Bobby drag the table out from behind the wood shed and set it under the weeping willow, where it was cooler. The lobsters took no time to boil and soon there was smacking and cracking of shells at the picnic table. No one spoke. They sucked the legs and cracked tails and big claws then dug in with their fingers. Freda collected the empty shells and tossed them into the garden.

When everyone was full, guests started to arrive. The Frickers and Warrens were over from North Bay, talking right away about the preparation of clam chowder with the Doyles and the Dauphinees from the Centre. They hovered near the big pot on the kitchen stove. Behind them, spread around the table, was a band of South Bayers. They held bottles of beer in their large hands, and each one wore a cap. Then the MacKinnons from the head of the Harbour were coming in. One had a guitar. Big happy fellows, these men; they took their jackets off, revealing the pale parts of their arms that had not been in the sun. Others from Neils Harbour and even the North Shore came. The last group, waitresses from the Keltic, arrived, and behind them Jimmy was ushered in. Someone screeched that the fiddle had arrived. Jimmy raised it high above his head to let Freda pass. Then he stood on a chair, the guitar player below him. With his head close to the ceiling, he began straight off, sawing into a batch of reels for the summer crowd.

Angus and his clippers showed up. Everyone moved aside to let him through. He had had a few drinks down at his house. Jimmy stopped playing, people stepped back.

Angus bellowed, "All right! Who needs the cut?" People laughed with relief. The electric cord of the hair clippers swung and bounced as he displayed his machine to everyone. Jimmy took off into an-other tune, a fast one, and this sent heat to the blood in Angus's limbs. He lifted his workboots to come down hard on Freda's lino-leum. Everyone was hooting in approval. He secured his clippers in the front pocket of his flannel shirt and pulled his sister from the crowd and out on the floor while the electric cord snapped and whipped at people, coming frighteningly close to the faces of some.

Freda pushed him back after the reel because tears filled her eyes. She had to catch her breath. Jimmy stopped. "I need a smoke!" he said. A beer was passed up to him, and he held its coolness lovingly against his face. He stepped down off the chair, which was then moved to the centre of the kitchen for the haircut. Angus had his clippers ready. Jorge was called upon, and smiling, came with arms lowered. But shouts were raised just before he sat, so he lifted his arms like a triumphant boxer. Someone caught Angus' cord and plugged it into an outlet.

"Fire up the music again, Jimmy," said Angus. "I'll need it for the shaving!" The crowd cheered, so Jimmy took up his fiddle and asked if the guitar player knew a particular set he wanted to play. He didn't.

"I'll play the haircut in the kitchen jig then," said Jimmy, and when he struck at the strings with his bow he began to invent the tune. This only enhanced the excitement, and the guitarist joined in.

Angus trimmed and clipped and made alterations; indeed, his face took on the look of profound concentration. He would look at the crowd occasionally and make faces. People would call out things, but he would not bat an eye at this. Jorge sat still, blinked the dry, smelly clippings off his lashes or drew out his lower lip and blew upwards to remove bits of hair from his face. Jimmy had stopped and was looking on.

Finally, Angus was finished. The watchful mob moved in to view the results. "I bald?" said Jorge looking up, his face looking youthful with such a short haircut.

"No," someone said. "You're Jorge. But you might wish you were bald!"

Another said, "Me son, thur's more hair on the forehead of a rattlesnake!"

A mirror was brought forward, and Jorge looked at his reflection.

He said to Angus that he thought it might be the best haircut he ever had.

"In time, you might really mean that," someone said.

"Yes, after about a year or two!"

Harold had arrived and was hollering for a broom and dust pan.

"Hair!" he said. "Thur's nothing worse for going all through the house! It's way, way worse than mussel shells! Give me the broom, I'll do it myself."

The music started louder than ever, and with more fury this time. Wilena was up out of her chair, dancing, the better part of a cigarette sticking straight out from clamped lips. Little blows of smoke came out her nose. Freda danced over to her, took the smoke, had a couple of puffs, then set it back in Wilena's mouth. They clutched hands and spun each other round. Tet-Yin rose, put his big arms around the two women, and they moved in circles around the floor. Jimmy, sweating heavily, was bowing near the bridge of the instrument, where the music was loudest. The guitar player, in the same spirit, beat the strings over the sound hole because the notes came fuller and deeper there. The kitchen was alive, a contented monster of music and dance and drink.

At the right time, near midnight, the crowd started to drop off. Freda went around making sure that anyone who had too much to drink was not behind the wheel of a car. Gloria, who had recently come up from the house, ferried a few home in hers. Others had set out on foot. The two community taxis were called and many went home in these. Abandoned cars lined the front drive. Freda switched off the porch light and left the yard in darkness.

Tet-Yin, Wilena, Jorge, Bobby, and Jimmy were left in the kitchen. They sat and talked infrequently, lightly. Jimmy had his shirt off, so Jorge and Bobby peeled theirs off, too. Tet-Yin, the last to strip down this way, announced that he wanted a tattoo, and everyone cracked up.

CHapteR 14

A week later Tet-Yin and Freda were at the Sydney Airport with
Wilena, Bobby, and Jorge. Freda had announced the morning after
the party that she and Tet-Yin would go back to Vancouver soon,
and a telephone call to the agent in Sydney meant they all could
travel together.

Once the five had boarded the plane and were strapped in, Freda
and Tet-Yin began to reminisce about the wonderful summer they
had had. But they agreed it would be good to get back to Vancouver.
Tet-Yin talked privately to Freda about his plans for the coming winter, and about returning to the Clyburn River next summer. Freda sat
in a lazy state and only smiled at all of this. It wasn't long before the
plane was setting everyone down on a Vancouver runway.

Late evening and the air was hot. The five continued in a taxi
downtown and said their goodbyes on Cardero Street. Freda and
Tet-Yin took their things and walked silently into their apartment.
Switching on the light, they saw all their possessions just as they
had left them, but the place looked strange to them. Freda opened a
window. Apartments are not houses, she thought. A house takes time
to acquaint yourself with, the apartment is known immediately.
There's still home in it, though. She opened a new package of tea.

"We don't have to see your daughter tonight, do we? I'm played
right out."

"I will go there. You don't have to, but I like."

They had a quick cup of tea, and Freda reminded herself to buy garlic in the morning. She had neglected it in Ingonish. When their cups were in the sink, they pulled on their light jackets and went to Tet-Yin's daughter.

Tet-Yin immediately freed blasts of pent-up Chinese when they arrived. Freda expected that he was talking about his summer or the garden, which they left in the hands of Jimmy and Gloria to harvest. He stopped at points to translate for her, but she told him not to bother, and began to talk to Pei-Jung instead.

On the way home, Tet-Yin took Freda's hand. They swung their arms as they walked. Warm air came in gusts down Cardero Street, trying to coax gum wrappers and dead leaves out of drains. It is nice here, thought Freda, as they continued along slowly. Her strongest wish, however, was to lay out flat and shut her eyes.

*

"Did I tell you he'd be let off? Did I?" Wilena had called to say that the verdict had been announced.

"What channel's it on?"

"All of them."

Freda found the remote control and turned to the same coverage as Wilena. The two talked about the crowds outside the courtroom and about the comments from individuals in the crowd.

"Enough of this," said Wilena. She switched off her TV. "As if anything else was going to happen."

Freda turned the volume down. "So are you coming to this film festival thing with us or not, Wilena? It's supposed to be here just the one time. That's what they're saying, anyway."

"If more fools like us believe it, they should make a killing! Yes, I got my pass. I got it yesterday. The size of the guide magazine they give a person! You're expected to sort through that to find the movies you want to see? I had a look. Most of them are about fruits or lizzies. What's going on with the world, Freda?"

"I know. They got as much of a story as anyone else, though, I suppose."

"What about us, Freda, real people, you and me? Perhaps they'll make a film about us one day."

"No, that's a show we'll have to enjoy in private, thank God."

"Hang on, I got the thing right here…Yes, it says here that one is about a story that takes place in Cape Breton. About mining."

"Pining?"

"Mining, you deaf fool!"

They made plans to meet before the film started and said good-bye. Freda got up to look out the window. A big wet leaf dropped from above and rain hit in a heavy shower against the side of the building. She drew the curtains, and looked at the calendar hanging on the wall. It was October.

Freda and Tet-Yin were in their apartment. Outside it was both a sunny and a rainy day. The window showed the street.

"This weather is call the Wedding of the Fox in Japan," said Tet-Yin.

"Why is that?"

"I don't know. My Grandfather could speak Japanese. When the sun and rain is outside like this he always say that." Tet-Yin was holding a set of blinds. He had a chair beside him and had already screwed in the top horizontal piece that would hold them. Wind came and spattered the window with large drops of rain.

"Well, we measured," said Freda. "They should just snap in there."

Tet-Yin got up on the chair.

"Now don't fall."

"Wha?"

"Don't fall! I said, and quit talking like you're from Cape Breton. All's I heard since coming back is wha, wha, wha."

Tet-Yin was on his toes. He was reaching but the blinds didn't fit.

"Leave it," said Freda. "Just hold still a minute while I go over

these instructions again. I don't know why I ever let you talk me
into blinds. I could have made curtains."

"Wha? Curtain?"

"Do you ever hear anything I say? Do you? We're gonna need
communication for this to work."

"For what work."

"For us to work."

"Also respect," said Tet-Yin into the window, poised and staring
off as a man at sea would.

"What do you mean, respect?" said Freda, the instructions rolled
up and in a dropped hand now.

"I mean you shout at me while I stand here. Is respect this?"

Tet-Yin was looking down over the blinds as if peering over a
bathroom stall. "Communication is for sure important but respect
also. You always say, easy, wait. Maybe I not ready. Well, when you
ready, Freda? You are independent woman, I know, but try depend-
ant woman sometime. This is respect. Let go. I do for you. I have
many thing happen before, everyone have. Tell me the difference
between independence and selfish. Tell me." Tet-Yin slowed down.

He lowered the blinds and turned his face away. Freda saw just a
part of his face. The colour had risen high in it. Hers must look the
same, she thought—the heat from anger, something a child wears.
She reached up and touched Tet-Yin's hand.

"I don't know what prompted all this, but come down. Come
on, I want to tell you something."

He got off the chair and turned his face toward hers.

"All of what you said is true you know."

Elevating his chin, Tet-Yin braced himself, as if not sure what was
coming next. Freda tilted her head into his shoulder and hugged him
close to her. She shut her eyes. Tet-Yin better positioned himself and
took her into himself too. The rain flicked onto the window and when
Freda opened her eyes she was almost certain she saw the same woman
with the dirty fur collar jacket looking at them from the street.

The sun shone down and lit the street nicely.

"All right, Tets, enough of this love making, let's get these blinds up before the whole world is gawking in at us."

Freda kept an eye on the street a moment where the leaves twisted on the trees.

*

The rain did not let up. During the next two weeks it came down steadily, and the streets were full of water. Freda, Tet-Yin, and Wilena experienced it first-hand in lineups, looking out from beneath umbrellas. And when they were not out in it, they were in darkened, damp movie theatres all over downtown Vancouver. They had daytime passes, which entitled them to watch as many films as they wanted between nine and six. Since the passes were expensive, they got up early, went out early, found the location of the films they wanted to see, and took breaks only for a brief lunch when the morning's film ended. As the days went by, not only their pants and shoes but their enthusiasm took a good soaking. They were getting through it, though. The festival was near its end.

They had taken turns choosing which films they would see. Although the films were mostly bad, the ribbing they gave the chooser made the experience enjoyable, especially when it came to Tet-Yin. The films he picked were from Vietnam, Thailand, China, England, Germany, South Africa, and other places the women had not even heard of. One film was from Korea. It was about two women who were next door neighbours, a fat one and a skinny one; the fat one ended up eating the skinny one.

"What sickens me most is the ones in these lineups," Wilena was saying one day while they waited for her choice. "They go on and on about the movies. It's thur whole life. It's all they live for. They probably follow these things all over the country, watching every movie they can. Imagine if they ever stopped watching and did a bit of living on their own for a change! Listen to them. They got it all figured out. They stand in these wet lineups waiting for the next one and say, 'I think the last film was vague. I think it lacked plot.' Hard life isn't it, sitting, watching and talking about what they see on a screen."

"Wilena, for the love of God. They're looking."

"They can look all they want, think I care? I'm tired of having to listen to them!"

The lineup began moving, and they found three seats together. The movie was called "Margaret's Museum" and the theatre was packed to the rafters.

"Go drain your bladder," Freda said to Tet-Yin. "Go now so you don't have to disturb us like you always do." Tet-Yin got up but was back in time for the lights to go out. The big wide screen lit up all the faces in the theatre. Tet-Yin took Freda's hand during the movie.

When the film ended, most of the audience stood and began applauding. It had been a good one, there was no denying it. Wilena turned to her friends.

"Who picked this one? Me, that's who. Twenty-seven that makes it, but we had to go through twenty-six till we came to one worth watching."

The three found their way out of the theatre and listened to snatches of movie analyses. This time they wanted to hear it, and it was all favourable.

*

In all her life, Freda had never had to rent a boat. In Ingonish, boats dotted the shore and when you wanted to go out in one, you only needed to ask a friend. Tet-Yin wanted to take his fishing rod out on the water before it got too cold and the winter set in, but who knew anyone with a boat in Vancouver?

They left from Granville Island after buying pumpkin pie to go with their sandwiches. Halloween was not far off, so of course the market at Granville had farmers' produce piled high on the tables. Freda had gone to a woman to pay for her pie after choosing a good one. The cashier pushed the change down into her palm in a most unfriendly manner. Freda told herself to forget it, that the woman was just busy. But the bad feeling persisted. She told Tet-Yin how she felt. She acknowledged that it was a little thing, but hurtful all the same.

"Wherever you go there have people like this," he said. "They are just unhappy." She stopped thinking about it, because she didn't want it to ruin her whole day.

They motored away from the crammed floating wharfs below the market, with their pumpkin pie and their egg-and-cheese sandwiches. Freda considered throwing the pie in the water. She was sitting at the stern, near Tet-Yin's fishing gear. He was captain. He said he had operated bigger boats than this in Hong Kong. Freda believed him, because the boat was about half the size of a living room, with a motor. She kept an eye out as Tet-Yin negotiated past the many wharfs and docked boats; the channel they were leaving was very narrow, but they made it out.

Relaxing a little, she crossed her legs, leaned back, and lit a cigarette. She hauled in hard on the smoke. It gave her a sharp awareness out here on the water. The taste of the seasalt was on her lips. The motor was making a sucking sound deep under her seat, at the stern. She took another drag. Hell, she had good lungs, there was no question of that. Why worry? Smoking might even give her an edge somehow, enhance things. Why the hell not? People did what they did, otherwise what kind of world would it be?

Tet-Yin had his knees bent to gain balance at the wheel. He steered deliberately, as if he were a man who had spent his entire life tracing coastlines—a cartographer, one who had never once gotten out of his boat, but did his work by feel. He had told Freda that he and his father had operated sampans and tugboats. Oh, she believed that all right; it was just the size that she had to make adjustments for when he told her things. She imagined him in one of the numerous tidy boats in that bay scurrying here and there, busy making a great mess of everything between Kowloon and Hong Kong, not leaving the poor water alone—the one time he was out.

"Don't forget your watch!" she hollered.

He did not hear. Probably thinking of the days when he was second mate to his father. Oh, that motor's loud. Daylight savings today. An hour of light will be gone today, hour hands go back, time lost—quite a concept, that is. She raised her cigarette to her lips. As if time could be saved, lost, taken, or gained. She squinted her eyes.

The sun was a perfect ball where it was, above their little boat. All alone, undisturbed, they had a whole blue sky to sail free in. A few other fishing boats were out, tiny ones like theirs, some motoring, others calm in the tide of English Bay. Tet-Yin wanted to go to Bowen Island, a little place just across from Horseshoe Bay. He had gone there when first arriving in British Columbia and discovered a good restaurant there. They would have an early supper, if they felt like it.

Freda twisted the end of her cigarette into the wood of the boat. There was still a lot left, but she didn't mind. She set the butt down in an empty bucket near her and put on the life jacket she had been sitting on till now. She did not do it up but, folding her arms over the long straps, she dropped her head to stare at the time on her watch. Tet-Yin cut the motor.

With his first fishing rod set and leaning out over a gunwale, he worked on getting the second rod together for Freda. He let her take care of the hook. She was a little reluctant taking the fishing rod from him because her hands were cold, but when she had the night crawler on and her hands on the dry cork of the handle— the line and weight bouncing out at the end of the rod—she became more interested.

They drifted toward shore and when they were at a good distance from it, Tet-Yin tossed the anchor. Their hooks were in the water, and the boat felt solid where it sat.

The raw air produced a pallor on Tet-Yin's face. His lips were the colour of the night crawlers. Out here on the water, in the lifting and falling of the boat's deck, Freda noticed the differences between them: his yellow skin, his flat nose, the roundness of his head and hands, the black, black eyes.

They fished for over an hour. There were no bites, and the lines got slimy with seaweed scum. They locked their reels and secured their rods against the side of the boat, and ate their sandwiches. Freda got out the thermos of coffee that Tet-Yin had brought and poured it into two plastic cups.

The boat was pulling harder at the anchor line. A breeze was up and over them now. The two sat on the raised part of the boat in the shadow of the cabin roof. The coffee was sweet.

"Ya put too much frigging sugar in this. I can feel the cavities starting already. You'll hafta take me to see a dentist before we even get there."

He looked at her trying to understand. Poor Tet-Yin, she thought. Has he really understood anything of my world? Here he sits, so happy to be here with me.

"We go to Bowen Island now."

He stood up, went to the stern and hauled on the anchor rope, the cold line immediately going tight in his hands. Freda watched. His hands worked the rope like an old bear yanking out a small tree.

"Shouldn't you start the boat first?"

He tried to turn, to look, to see what she had said, but before he could get around his leg came out from under him and he dropped hard on the deck. His head made a nasty sound against the gunwale and the line of the anchor pulled back through his loosened hands.

"Oh, dear Jesus! You all right?" Freda had jumped up and was beside him. His eyes were closed, the right corner of his lips raised. His breathing sounded terrible. She had her face down beside his and could smell a sweetness in his breath.

"I…I…Wa la wei—"

"Shush. Easy, easy. Hang on…" She knew what this was. She had taken him to the doctor about it, but it was supposed to be nothing. Yes, a heart is nothing.

"Can you get up?"

"No cannot. Freda…No, I…"

She let him be, found a blanket in a compartment below and laid it over him. It covered him, but was not thick enough.

"What do I do? You tell me!"

"Begin the boat, Freda. Okay, okay, can."

She left him and went up to the controls and pushed the button near the steering wheel. It was dark purple, the colour of his lips. Oh, Christ Almighty! You stupid, stupid bastard! She looked all around, at the sun, at the water. She wanted something or someone to see.

The motor turned over and started, but there was a pathetic grinding and gurgling, not the usual noise. She looked at the shore and saw houses on it, but they were too far away. The shore itself, however, was not. They were adrift, and they would be up on the rocks if she didn't do something. She looked at the anchor line. It was taut, but not catching. She heard a cracking below in the shallows now—the propeller blades mixing up in something. She switched off the motor and could hear the quiet of the wind and feel it over her face.

"Hang on! Oh, hang on, will ya," she shouted back, above sore bent knees. Letting go of the wheel, she pulled hard and slow at the anchor rope. Her pulling brought them out into deeper water, above where the anchor was now caught. She tried the engine again. To the side, through a small Plexiglass window in the cabin, she could see the big Bowen Island ferries moving neatly and high across the strait. They were not so far away but, like floating mountains, the things sailed onward and could pay no attention. People stood on the decks, in the cold bright sun, their hair twisting in the wind.

The engine caught but it sounded different again. Something had been shorn off. She pushed up the throttle to full speed, but the boat only wormed ahead. The anchor! Cursed old Christ! Is this all meant to happen this way?

She let the engine idle and angrily pulled at the slow, taut anchor line. There was so much rope to it. When it was up far enough, she gave a sudden heave and the anchor broke the surface. She threw it into the mess of rope now over the bottom of the boat.

They went in a slow spin, circling like a half-dead shark. Freda went to the wheel and tried it, but there was still something wrong. The boat would only go round slowly, steadily. Something had surely come off her. Jesus, Jesus! Her mind raced through the possibilities: a propeller blade, a rudder piece, and clip, a pin. Who in the miserable old cursed fuck knows!

"You take it easy there now," she called to Tet-Yin. "Are ya listening? Are ya?"

She put her strength into the throttle to increase the speed, and something caught, making them go straighter. She could feel it in her hands. Even with the speed, though, it only trickled ahead, nothing like before. She kept talking back to Tet-Yin, twisting her head around to do it. She had to keep her hands on the wheel because if she let go of it, the whole thing would turn astray again. She hollered some more.

"Answer me! Answer me!"

His ears are bad with this motor, she told herself, especially with this wind up and me standing here with my back to him. Jesus, Jesus, Jesus!

It was four o'clock. She let go of the steering wheel. Please God, give me a hand here. The boat began a turn; she rushed back to her post. She was messing up. She knew she had to stay where she was, had to take them tiredly in through this long choppy field of water. Her neck was sore from twisting to get a look at her husband.

Her life-jacket was on the floor, tangled up at her feet. She wondered how it had got there. Reaching down and taking its straps, she tried tying off the wheel, fastening the straps to one of the wooden supports running up the side of the forecastle. But they were too short. She kicked at the anchor rope; squatting, she grabbed it. Much better. She tied while keeping her hip and breast against the wheel. But she couldn't get it tight enough. I can't do it! It's still too loose, it needs strength and I haven't got it! To hell with it, then. She let the boat go completely and went back to Tet-Yin.

"Can you say something?"

"Wa, I...I am sorry, Freda."

"Sorry for what? Shush now. Just stay still for me. Can you do that?"

"Can."

She got to her feet but the unsteadiness of the vessel made walking difficult. She went into the forecastle, knowing there must be a radio or a flare.

She found the radio, switched it on and spoke into it. Nothing came back, and the spinning of the boat was really scaring her now. She stepped to the wheel, pointed them back towards the way they had come. She wanted only to get them in.

*

Five o'clock, and to all the rest of the natural universe, theirs was a small boat motoring leisurely, slicing through gentle, late October waves. Freda's neck, burning from twisting between Tet-Yin and her course, was straight now as she was scanning for nearby boats. Tears came and she could taste their salt in her mouth, and when the wind brushed across her cheeks she felt her skin tighten where the streams had dried.

There was still plenty of sun when the motor quit for good. There was a spare tank of gas, a full one, but she knew the rotting smell of a burnt battery—it was the one thing she did know. She was back with Tet-Yin, ladylike beside him, his head in her lap. The boat lifted and dropped, lifted and dropped. They talked about things, about what to do with him if they didn't make it back in time. The anchor rope was tangled everywhere hanging off the wheel, strung up near the cabin's roof, and where it held the steering mechanism, it snapped back and forth now with a clicking sound, back and forth like a pendulum. Underneath the boat, the rudder board moved freely, ceaselessly, in the current.

Six o'clock, by daylight savings time.

A deep horn blared from a passing tanker. Then for one, long moment, a cold band of black shadow darkened Freda and Tet-Yin's little boat.

The sun had just about disappeared from English Bay when someone called down from a docked ocean liner to Freda in her boat. Her vessel pressed like a wine cork up against the steel of the huge hull. Its tiny sides gnashed the liner's pock of barnacles, chewing them to chalk.

A world of steel towered above Freda. The voice of the tugboat operator sounded out from behind, and when the tugboat got close enough, its man boarded the little boat. The operator spoke to Freda, but she did not seem to see or hear him. He saw what the trouble was, then, and tied their boats together in silence as quickly as he could. He radioed to the boat owner and gave him the news.

Along the Seawall now, Freda was thinking, at shore, no one sat on any of the donated benches. It was all empty, dark, and full of shadows.

Wilena was on the dock when they were bringing them in. The owner had called her when his boat did not come back in. Freda had put her friend's name and number down as an emergency contact.

Wilena saw Freda sitting at attention at the stern of the tugboat. Anyone else would have mistaken her for a piece of equipment, some tool or machine that was part of the boat.

They loaded Tet-Yin into an ambulance and took him away. Freda
was in the arms of Wilena, who had to reach up to get a good hold
on her friend. Bobby drove them to Wilena's apartment, and the
women were up the whole night. Freda lay on the chesterfield, an
afghan pulled up to her neck. Her grey hair hung over the bright
colours of the blanket. Her face was stony, bare.

"How tough do you have to be?" she said out to Wilena at one
point in the night.

"It's just what life wants from us sometimes."

"Well, I had enough of what life wants a long time ago. Do you
know that?"

"Me too," said Wilena. "Me too."

At the funeral, the Philippino priest said some beautiful words.
English Victoria cried her eyes out. Jorge did not raise his head.
Bobby's and Wilena's arms were at Freda's side, and they supported
their friend through it all. Pei-Jung and her family wore glasses over
puffy, sore eyes when they lowered him into the ground. He wanted
it this way, he had told Freda on the boat when he knew.

Freda stayed by the grave when the family had gone. She was
wearing a dress of Wilena's. She touched its material, then bent to
place the rose at the head of the grave. The earth was sodden with
rain, but it was drier near the head of the grave, where the shovels
first went in.

Freda found herself outside of her apartment building later, looking in. The curtains were drawn at her window. How can I go inside?
she thought. She walked up to the entrance and pulled open the heavy
door. She went into their apartment and looked at the light she had
left on. It was coming from a small lamp on an end table. With her
coat on, she went over to it and sat, dripping rain into the sofa and
onto the rug. She folded her arms, and began to weep.

A few minutes later she stood and went to the window. She
peeked between the drapes and saw the rain pulling on the few dead
leaves that still clung to branches. It drowns life out here, she

thought; it just pours down from the heavens. Nothing to be done about it. She let go of the curtains, lifted the telephone receiver, and dialled Wilena.

"Hi. I'm not doing so well."

"You're not supposed to be."

"What am I supposed to be?" Freda knew what her friend was going to say, and she breathed quietly, waiting to hear it.

"Strong," she said. "Strong, dear, strong."